The Children Next Door

Laura wrenched open the gate as far as it would go and squeezed herself out on to the pavement. There she had a shock: the road was completely empty! Not a car, a lorry, not even a motor bike. And not a sign of the three children.

She stood for a moment, unable to believe it. People couldn't disappear just like that! If there had been an accident, someone would have had to call an ambulance; they wouldn't simply have bundled all three of them into a car and driven off. And if there hadn't been an accident, then why hadn't they come back?

Hippo Ghost

The Children Next Door

Jean Ure

Scholastic Children's Books,
Scholastic Publications Ltd,
7-9 Pratt Street, London NW1 0AE

Scholastic Inc.,
555 Broadway, New York, NY 10012-3999, USA

Scholastic Canada Ltd,
123 Newkirk Road, Richmond Hill,
Ontario, Canada L4C 3G5

Ashton Scholastic Pty Ltd,
P O Box 579, Gosford, New South Wales,
Australia

Ashton Scholastic Ltd,
Private Bag 92801, Penrose, Auckland,
New Zealand

First published in the UK by Scholastic Children's Books 1994
This edition published by Scholastic Children's Books 1995

Copyright © Jean Ure 1994

ISBN 0 590 55833 1

Typeset by A J Latham, Houghton Regis, Dunstable, Beds

Printed and bound in Great Britain by
Cox & Wyman Ltd, Reading, Berkshire

10 9 8 7 6 5 4 3 2 1

For Norm and Adèle

Chapter One

Laura was lying stretched out on her front in the garden, reading a book, when she heard the children's voices. In fact, to be honest, she had fallen asleep over her book – it was about people from olden times and full of language that she didn't always understand – and the children's voices had woken her.

She rolled over on to her side, propping herself on an elbow, and listened. First of all she heard a girl's voice – "Tommy! Leave off! You're hurting me!" – and then a boy's, which sounded younger: "You gimme back my Rollsy!"

"Shan't! I told you! It's a road hog!"

"It's not a road hog. It's just *faster*."

The voices were coming from the other side of the fence. Laura sat up properly and strained her ears to hear.

"If you want me to play with you, you'll have to obey the rules."

"Piddle to the rules!"

"*Tommee*! I'll tell Ma you said that!"

"Tell her, then! Tell-tale! Girls are always tell-tales." There was a pause, then: "Specially *sisters*."

"For that you jolly well won't get your Rollsy back!"

A small object came hurtling over the fence and landed in the middle of a large pink bush. (Laura didn't know the name of the bush. She wasn't very good, yet, with things that grew. For eleven years she had lived with her mum and dad in a flat in the middle of London, almost on top of King's Cross station, where the only flowers she had seen were the bulbs that her mum kept indoors or the bunches they sold from barrows in the street.)

From the other side of the fence came a loud howl of anguish.

"*Em!* That was my *Rollsy*!"

"It was your own fault. You asked for it."

There was a note of bravado in the girl's voice, but at the same time she did sound a bit ashamed. And so she should, thought Laura, shocked. Fancy throwing her little brother's toy away!

Laura herself was an only child; she would have loved more than anything to have a brother or sister. She couldn't imagine ever quarrelling with them, especially if they were smaller than she was. She pictured a tiny, curly-headed boy bursting into tears, and yes, sure enough, there he went! The sound of piteous weeping could now be heard through the fence.

Laura was about to scramble to her feet and go running over to the pink bush to search for the lost Rollsy when she heard the girl, rather gruffly, say, "Oh, I suppose I'll have to get it back for you!" and the next second, to her astonishment, a pair of hands appeared at the top of the fence followed almost immediately by a head.

The head had to belong to the girl called Em. She was about Laura's age (which was eleven years and two months) with a round, cheerful face, pink-cheeked and brown-eyed. Her hair, which was dark chestnut, was in two long plaits tied with red ribbons.

Em looked quickly down the garden, then up towards the house. She didn't see Laura, probably because the apple tree cut off her line of vision. Laura, who was shy, instinctively shrank behind it. She wished afterwards that she had been braver, but

Laura spent her life wishing that. She was what her gran called "a quiet little soul", which meant that she was always missing out on things because of being too bashful to put herself forward.

If she had behaved like a normal girl, instead of a silly timid quivering thing, hiding behind an apple tree in her own back garden, she might have made a new friend. As it was, Laura continued to crouch and shrink whilst Em boldly hoisted herself astride the fence, leaped down on the other side and began vigorously grubbing about amongst the pink foliage.

She looked like the sort of girl it might have been fun to be friends with. She was wearing pleated navy blue shorts and a blue short-sleeved blouse rather like the one that Laura was going to have to wear for gym and PE at the new school that she was starting in September. Her legs were bare and brown and her feet were pushed into ordinary common-or-garden plimsolls. Laura noted the plimsolls specially. Her gran had said only the other week that "Plimsolls were considered quite good enough in my day. We didn't expect our parents to fork out hard-earned cash on pairs of fancy trainers." Her gran would approve of a girl who wore plimsolls.

The little boy's head now popped up over the fence.

"Can you find it, Em?"

The little boy looked angelic – exactly the sort of brother that Laura would have liked to have. His face was round, like his sister's, but pinker and chubbier, and his hair was curly, just as she had imagined it would be. She thought that he was probably about six years old.

"Em! Is it there?"

Em's voice rose, impatiently, from out of the pink bush.

"I'm looking!"

Laura longed – she really *did* long – to go over and help her, but nobody could ever guess the torments that went on in Laura's mind. Other girls simply walked up to people and said hallo. Laura couldn't. She had to think about it and think about it until it was too late, which was what happened now. Just as she had screwed up enough courage to come out from behind her apple tree a sharp, angry female voice cried, "Clear off, you children!"

Laura sprang round to see where the voice was coming from, but there didn't seem to be anyone. It had sounded as if it came from the kitchen window, but it certainly wasn't her mum. It must have been someone from the small block of flats next door; some crabby old woman who didn't like children, though what it had to do with her Laura couldn't imagine. After all, they were in Laura's garden, not hers.

She turned back again just in time to see

the tail end of Em disappearing over the fence. Tommy had already gone. She heard his voice, wailing: "I want my Rollsy!"

"I'll get you another one, Tommy. Honest!"

"You won't! You can't! That one was special!"

"I'll save up my pocket money, even if it takes me months."

"But it won't be the same!"

"No, it'll be better, 'cos it'll be new."

"I want *my* one!"

"I'll tell you what," said Em, "we'll wait till Kate's here and then we'll have another look … a proper one, this time."

There was a silence, and Laura thought the children had gone. She crept forward towards the fence, and then she heard snuffling, and Tommy's voice, miserable: "Kate's not coming for ages."

"She is, too! She's coming for a weekend before we go back to school."

"Wh–" Tommy hiccuped – "when's that?"

"September. That means –" a pause, while Em (presumably) counted on her fingers – "that means there's only another five weeks to go, and Kate'll be here before that."

"*When*?"

"End of August, that's when."

More doleful sniffing, then Tommy's voice, fainter now, as they moved towards the house, "I hope it doesn't rain … I don't want Rollsy to get wet."

Laura ran across the garden towards the pink shrub. She would find the little boy's Rollsy for him! And then perhaps she would be brave enough to take it round to him and maybe Em would be there and maybe Em would ask her in and they would talk about which schools they were both going to and what bliss if it turned out that Em was going to the same one as Laura!

Laura was dreading the start of the new school term. Her mum said that she would have had to be starting at a new school anyway, now that she was eleven, but at least if they'd stayed in King's Cross she would have moved on with people she knew. At Turnham Green (which was still London, but not right in the middle) she wouldn't know a single soul.

She had reached the pink bush, but to her dismay it was surrounded by a thicket of horrible prickly brambles. Even Laura could recognize a bramble. The whole garden was overgrown, with dandelions and stinging nettles and creeping stuff which her gran said was ground ivy.

"I don't envy you that," Gran had said. "Gets everywhere, ground ivy."

The house had stood empty for almost eighteen months before Laura's mum and dad had bought it. There was ivy (the climbing kind, not the creeping sort) growing all up the walls and over the windows, and indoors the rooms had smelt of must and old plaster. The house had been built a hundred years ago. It was tall and narrow, and the garden was long and narrow. Laura was sure there must be ghosts, but Mum hadn't liked that idea and Gran had pooh-poohed it.

"No such thing as ghosts!"

There might not have been such things as ghosts (though Laura privately believed that ghosts probably *did* exist), but there were certainly such things as brambles. Laura fell back, defeated, sucking at her thumb where a thorn had jabbed her. Brambles were painful. She wondered how Em had ever managed to find a way in. She had seemed to crawl underneath, but Laura couldn't see how – especially with bare arms and legs. Em was obviously a lot tougher than Laura. On the other hand, she *had* lost her little brother's Rollsy so it was only right she should have braved the brambles.

Laura thought that some time, when her dad wasn't busy doing other things, she would ask him if they could clear the brambles away, then she would be able to look properly.

She wandered down the brick path (you could just see the bricks through the ground ivy) to the bottom of the garden. It was dark and damp right down at the bottom. Rather spooky. A line of tall fir trees cut out all the light, and under the fir trees nothing grew, not even ground ivy. Just in front of the trees, by the fence, were the remains of an old shed. The shed had long since collapsed, and so had the fence behind it. By clambering over the rotting timber, on which all kinds of weedy things were growing, Laura found that she could see into next door's garden.

It was long and narrow, like her own. There was a gate at the bottom, and a compost heap, and several rows of vegetables, including some that climbed up poles and some that looked like green cauliflowers. Then there was a sandpit, where the children obviously played, and a home-made swing – just a plank of wood and two lengths of rope – hanging from the branch of a tree. Then there was some trellis, with an archway, and roses growing over it, and beyond that Laura couldn't see because the trellis was too high.

She slithered down again, over the pile of weeds and timber, and walked back, frowning, up the path. She had been quite happy (before she had fallen asleep) reading her book about the olden days people. She liked reading books.

"Lives in a world of her own," her gran always said.

But books weren't her world, they were worlds that had been created by other people. Her world was here, in this garden, at number 44 Hindes Road, Turnham Green. And her world was *empty*.

Why, oh why, hadn't she been brave enough to speak to Em while she had the chance?

* * *

That evening over tea, when her dad was home, Laura said: "There are two children living next door."

"Really?" said her mum. "I thought it was just an old lady."

"There *is* an old lady," said Laura, "but I think she lives in the flats."

"How do you know?" Her dad sounded surprised. It wasn't like Laura to know about the neighbours. She was so shy she usually hid herself away rather than say good morning to anyone.

"I heard her," said Laura. "She was shouting at the children."

Laura's mum and dad looked at each other. Laura's mum, very faintly, shook her head. Her dad said, "Which children? Out in the road?"

"No! The ones next door … Tommy and Em."

"Tommy and Em?" Her mum shot another quick glance at Laura's dad. "You mean you actually spoke to them?"

"No." Laura blushed. She had a delicate, oval-shaped face with very pale ivory skin. She blushed easily. She had tried to grow her hair long so that she could shake it over her face like a curtain, as she had seen other girls do, but Laura's hair, though a pretty light brown, was annoyingly fine and wispy and didn't look good when it grew past her ears.

"So if you didn't speak to them," said her mum, "how do you know what their names are?"

"I heard them talking to each other." She wasn't going to say that Em had actually jumped over the fence. She didn't *think* her parents would be cross, because in general they weren't, but this was the first garden they'd ever had and they might not like the idea of strange girls leaping into it.

"Maybe they were visiting," said Mum. "Some time I must go and introduce myself. I'll find out for you."

That alarmed Laura: she didn't want anything *found out*. The children would think she had been spying on them if her mum went round asking questions.

"I was just saying," she said. "That's all."

*   *   *

The children didn't seem to be there next day, or if they were they didn't go out into the garden. Laura had set up a table under the apple tree and was there all morning and all afternoon, first of all doing a jigsaw puzzle and then doing some painting. She would have heard them if they had been there. (Her mum, thank goodness, was still busy setting the house to rights and didn't have time to go round asking questions and finding things out.)

Next day, Laura felt a bit feverish and sorry for herself as she sometimes did when her tonsils played up. Her mum put out the new lounger for her, under the apple tree in the shade, with lots of cushions and a blanket just in case she felt cold, and a tray with a jug of orange juice and her book about the olden times. If you had to have attacks of tonsils, it was at least better to have them in a garden, under an apple tree, than shut up in a poky fifth-floor flat near King's Cross.

"I'm just popping down the road to get a few things," said Laura's mum, after lunch. "Is there anything you want, and will you be all right left on your own for a short while?"

Laura said yes, she would be perfectly all right – Turnham Green wasn't King's Cross, and after all she *was* eleven and old enough to go to secondary school – and please could she have some lemon barley water for her throat?

While her mum was out, Laura dozed, and while she dozed she dreamt that Em had come back over the fence and that they were looking for the lost toy together. She was woken by the familiar sound of voices – happy, this time, and laughing; not quarrelling as they had before.

She lay for a while, half dozing, half listening. Where was Tommy? She couldn't hear his voice, only girls' voices. It must be Em and someone else.

Carefully, Laura swung herself off the lounger and tiptoed down the brick path, on wobbly legs, to the bottom of the garden, then crawled up the timber pile and cautiously peered over the broken palings of the fence. She would have died if anyone had seen her, but the two girls were fully absorbed in what they were doing, which was building a sandcastle in the sandpit. They had a big watering can, and a small spade and pail.

Laura – who had never been to the seaside – watched, fascinated, as they mixed up sand and water, filled the pail with it, then upended the pail and tipped out a perfectly formed mould which held together just as if it had been made of cement.

They were using the moulds to adorn the flat top of the castle. It was a very splendid castle; it even had a moat and a drawbridge. Em, who was wearing a short dress covered in a pattern of bright red flowers and had her hair tied on top of her head with a red ribbon, was the one who was mainly responsible for the sand pies. The other girl, who was wearing a blue dress, and a floppy sort of hat with a flap which covered the back of her neck, was engaged in stripping the petals off a yellow flower and spiking them on twigs to make flags for the sand pies. All the sand pies had little yellow flags flying from the tops of them. The other girl was gingery, with freckles and a sharp nose. Every now and again she would say something to Em, and Em would giggle and bat at her with the spade. Laura wished she knew what the giggles were about.

Of course, strictly speaking it was eavesdropping to squat on top of the ruined shed and listen in on other people's conversation, but she couldn't for the most part hear what they were saying so she didn't feel too badly about it. It wasn't until Tommy suddenly appeared, bursting through the archway in the rose-covered trellis and leaping into the sandpit like a small angry whirlwind, that Laura could hear.

"You beasts!" shouted Tommy. "You horrible rotten beasts! You and Kate ... I hate you both!"

So the gingery girl was Kate. Laura

looked at her, jealously. She wasn't supposed to have been coming yet. Not until the end of August, Em had said. Already Laura didn't like the idea of Em having another friend; for if Em had Kate, what were the chances of her wanting Laura? But maybe – she cheered up slightly – maybe the Kate girl lived a long way away and Em didn't see her very often.

Tommy, meanwhile, in a rage, was stamping about the sandpit, kicking sand in all directions.

"I hate you!" screamed Tommy.

The two girls looked at each other and pulled faces, lips pursed and eyebrows raised. They were making fun of him, Laura could see.

"Sneaking off without me! Without telling me!"

"There are moments – " Em upturned her pail and rapped it smartly with the back of the spade – "when one does not wish to play with six-year-olds."

"Thank you all the same," added Kate, wrenching another petal from her flower.

Tommy's face puckered and grew dangerously red.

"That's my bucket and spade you've got there!" He lunged forward and made a grab. Em neatly whisked them out of his way. "If I can't play, you can't use my things! You already lost my Rollsy!"

"Shut up!" said Em. "We looked for it, didn't we?"

"All over," said Kate.

Laura gasped. That was a lie! Unless they had climbed into the garden very early in the morning or very late in the evening, they hadn't been anywhere near the pink shrub and the patch of horrible snatching brambles. And she didn't think they *had* climbed over. She had looked again at the brambles and she hadn't seen any signs of anyone trampling on them or slashing at

them, which was what you would have to
do if you were to have a proper search.
Fancy telling lies to your own little brother!

"Anyway, I said," said Em. "I'll get you
another one."

"When?"

"Some time," said Em, beginning to fill
her pail with more sand and water.

"*When*?"

"When I've got the money! Just shove off
and leave us alone!"

Em raised her spade to give him a
thwack, but Tommy was too fast for her.
Ducking under her arm he flew at the sand
castle and began kicking at it, sobbing as he
did so.

"I hate you! I hate you both!"

Em shrieked and hit at him with the
spade. Kate cried, "Tommy, you utter pig!"

"I hate you, I hate you, I hate you!"
sobbed Tommy, running up the garden as
fast as his chunky legs would carry him. He

was pursued by Em with the spade and Kate with a twig. The cries faded into the distance, and suddenly the garden was empty.

Laura stood up, slowly and a little bit uncertainly. Her legs had gone all weak and watery from having squatted on her heels too long, and her head felt as if a swarm of bees were buzzing in it. That was her tonsils, giving her a high temperature. Just for a moment, as she stared down into the deserted garden, she thought she was at the seaside, which she had seen often enough on television even if she hadn't been there. She knew how the waves rippled and foamed as they came up the beach. That was exactly what the air was doing, now: rippling and foaming and making her feel quite giddy.

Step by step, Laura made her way back over the pile of timber, down the brick path and across the grass (which couldn't yet be called a lawn but might be when her dad had pulled up all the dandelions and ground ivy) and on to her lounger. She had just settled herself thankfully against the cushions when the back door opened and her mum appeared.

"Did you wonder where I'd got to? Have you been all right? I bumped into our next-door neighbour … Mrs Hobbs. She's staying there to look after her mother-in-law. Apparently the old lady's not too well. And there *is* a little girl, her name's Zilla. She's staying there with her mother and she's the same age as you. You've been invited round to tea on Friday, if you're feeling better. I said you probably would be. So – " Her mum beamed. "That's nice, isn't it? Someone to make friends with."

Laura pulled herself higher up against the cushions.

"What about Tommy and Em?"

Her mum frowned. Laura recognized it

as her warning frown. What it meant was, "Now, then, Laura! Don't let's start that."

Her mum thought she was making them up; either that or imagining them. Laura did imagine things – or at least, everyone said that she did. When she had lived in the flat near King's Cross she had complained that she couldn't sleep at night because of a baby that kept crying, but nobody in the flats around them had had a baby. The doctor had suggested that maybe she was scared of the dark (she was, a little bit) and another doctor, a more important one, had said that she was trying to draw attention to herself.

"She is obviously insecure."

She was that a little bit, as well; but she *knew* she had heard a baby crying, just as she knew she had seen Tommy and Em, playing.

"It's because you're on your own," said her mum, pouring her out a glass of lemon barley. "That's what it is. It'll be better when you've started school … I do hope you make some friends! It's a pity the little girl next door is only visiting. Still, I gather she's going to be here for the whole of the holidays, so that will be something. She's a nice little girl, and she's looking forward to meeting you."

Laura's heart drooped. She didn't want to meet this Zilla, whoever she was; she wanted to meet Em. She felt as though she already knew Em. It would be easy talking to her. She would tell her how she was going to ask her dad to cut the brambles down so that they could have a proper look for Tommy's Rollsy. And maybe Em would take her down the garden to play in the sandpit. It was probably a bit childish, to be making sand pies and building sand castles at the age of eleven, but Laura didn't mind. She liked childish things.

"When you've been to Zilla's," said her

mum, happily squashing her pillows into shape, "Zilla can come to you. Oh, and by the way, there aren't any old ladies living in the block next door. I asked Mrs Hobbs. There are only three flats and they're all taken by young couples."

It could have been someone's grandmother, thought Laura, but she didn't bother saying so. Her mum would only think she was imagining things and then she would start fussing and say "Oh, Laura, not that again!"

There were some things, reflected Laura, that were best kept to oneself.

Chapter Two

For the next two days it was dismal and rainy, and Laura's tonsils were still playing up, which meant she had to stay indoors, lying on the sofa with her lemon barley water and the television. As a rule her mum didn't let her watch television more than one hour a day, or two at weekends, but she always made an exception when she had her tonsils.

One day, probably, the tonsils were going to mean an operation. Laura didn't like the thought of that. People could die from operations, and Laura was scared of death. It was something she tried not to think about, though every now and again, in the middle of the night, she would wake up and start panicking. Suppose she were to die *now*, all by herself, with no one to say goodbye to her?

Secretly she was ashamed of these thoughts – they were what her gran called "morbid" – but somehow she couldn't seem to stop them. Once she had woken up and seen angels hovering over the bed, and another time she had frightened herself by imagining how it would be to be buried alive, lying wrapped up in the duvet until she almost couldn't breathe.

She would have liked to ask other people if they had the same sort of melancholy thoughts, but unfortunately it wasn't the sort of thing you could talk to anyone about. Her mum would only get upset, and other people, probably, would think she was mad.

On Friday when she woke up her tonsils had gone, and so had the rain. She was glad about the rain but wouldn't have minded having the tonsils for a bit longer. Today was the day she had been invited to tea with the girl next door – the Zilla girl. She wasn't looking forward to that. What would they find to talk about? What would they do? The Zilla girl was bound to think she was boring and wish she hadn't come.

"Have a nice time," said her mum, as she sent Laura off promptly at three o'clock. "Oh, and Laura … don't mention anything about the other two, will you? There's a good girl."

By the other two her mum meant Tommy and Em. She didn't know about Kate. But of course Laura wouldn't mention them, she would be far too shy. She probably wouldn't open her mouth all the time she was there, except to put food in, and even that was an embarrassment.

Laura always made sure to help herself to the tiniest of everything, and to avoid anything which looked as if it might crumble or squidge, because if anything *was* going to crumble or squidge then sure as eggs it would crumble all over the carpet and squidge all over the tablecloth and make the most horrible mess.

Laura pushed open the gate of number 42. The gate was old and heavy, and creaked like something out of a horror film. The whole of the front garden was a bit like a horror film. There were privet hedges towering several metres above her, and dark green laurel bushes pushing out all over the path. She knew they were laurels because number 44 had one. Her gran had said "Typical Victorian!"

Nervously, Laura raised the big iron knocker (it looked like a long black tongue) and tapped with it against the door. She thought, but couldn't be certain, that one of the curtains twitched at a downstairs window. This place was creepy!

Almost immediately the door was thrown open. The girl who stood there looked amazingly like Em. She had the same round cheerful face and brown eyes, though her hair, which was mouse rather than chestnut, was cut close to her head and curly. She was wearing red tights and a blue T-shirt and had a big grin stretching almost from one ear to the other.

"Just as well I was watching for you … you have to bash that knocker really *hard*."

"Not as hard as all that!" A lady appeared at the far end of the hallway. The hallway was as dark and gloomy as the front garden, with what looked like treacly brown lino stuck to the walls.

"Hallo, Laura!" The lady held out a hand, as if they were both grown ups. "It is Laura, isn't it? This is Zilla, and I'm her mum. Come in! And don't worry about bashing the knocker … the way Zilla goes at it we'll have a hole in the front door very soon!"

"But that's what it's there for," said Zilla. "To knock with."

"Precisely! To knock with. Not to bash with. Come on, Laura! Come through."

Zilla's mum led the way into the kitchen. It hadn't been modernized like the one at number 44. There was an old stone sink and a wooden draining board and shelves with hooks for the cups to hang on.

"Brilliant!" said Zilla. "Don't you think?"

"Like something out of the dark ages," said her mum.

"It's real antiques." Zilla said it proudly. "The whole house is an antique. Look!" She pointed at a glass-fronted box on the wall. "Those are the bells they used to ring for the servants. Every time anyone wanted a servant they'd press a button and a little light would flash down here in the kitchen."

"And some poor soul would have to go running. Lovely," said Mrs Hobbs, "so long as you weren't a servant."

"There's even a ghost," said Zilla. "It w– "

"We don't wish to hear about ghosts, thank you very much!" Zilla's mum gave her a little push towards the back door. "Why don't you take Laura in the garden for a bit? We'll have tea later on. I'll call you when it's ready."

"OK. Come on!" Zilla jerked her head at Laura, who followed meekly. "We've got a mangle out here. Would you like to see it?"

Laura struggled for a moment.

"What's a mangle?" she said.

"Something that mangles," said Zilla, making mangling motions with her hands. "It's round the back … I'll show you."

The mangle stood in a small dank outhouse. It had an iron frame and two long rollers, one under the other, close together, and a handle at the side.

"It's a Victorian torture machine," said Zilla. "What they used to do, they used to put people's fingers between the rollers and mangle them … like this, look!" Zilla picked up the edge of her T-shirt and began feeding it through the rollers, turning the handle as she did so. "It used to crush their bones."

Laura, being a serious sort of person, was never quite sure when other people were teasing her. She stared, doubtfully, at Zilla's T-shirt caught between the rollers.

"Now I'll *un*mangle myself," said Zilla, turning the handle back the other way. "Of course, you couldn't do that with fingers. Once they were crushed, they were crushed."

Laura swallowed.

"Is it really a torture machine?" she said.

"No! I told you! It's a mangle!" Zilla cackled. (Her laugh sounded uncannily like

Em's.) "Course it's not a torture machine, silly! It's what they used to put their wet clothes through to get the water out of them before they had tumble dryers. My gran still uses it."

Zilla led the way back into the garden. Laura was glad to be in the sunshine again.

"My gran's not very well," said Zilla. "That's why we're here, to look after her. We usually live somewhere else. Where did you live before you came here?"

"King's Cross," said Laura.

"King's Cross? That's a railway station! You can't live in a railway station!"

"We didn't live *in* the station." Laura said it carefully. "We lived *near* the station."

"We live near a station. It's not very nice, where we live. Turnham Green is heaps nicer. I wouldn't mind," said Zilla, "living here all the time." She slashed at some tall blue flowers spilling out of a flower bed. "I'm afraid the garden is rather untidy," said Zilla. "That's because my gran can't manage it any more."

"Wh – " Laura had turned quite pink with the effort of making conversation – "what's the matter with your gran?"

"She's going to die," said Zilla.

Laura stared at her, aghast. You just didn't *talk* about that sort of thing! Especially when it was your own gran.

"She's old," said Zilla. "If she lived till next year she'd be eighty. But my mum doesn't think she will. Mum says she doesn't want to. See, my granddad died when I was two, and my mum says Gran's never stopped missing him, so death will be a welcome release and it will be selfish if we cry. Mum says we ought to be glad for her."

There was a silence. Laura didn't know which way to look. She had never heard anyone be brazen enough to talk about death before. Even when Laura's guinea-pig had died Mum hadn't talked about it. One day he had been there and the next day he hadn't, and neither had his cage, and Mum had taken Laura to stay with Gran for a few days so that Laura wouldn't dwell on it.

"Much the best way," Mum had said.

But Bootsy, although Laura had loved him, had only been a guinea-pig. Zilla was talking about her *gran*.

Laura thought of her own gran. Gran certainly wasn't young, but she wasn't old, either. Not *old* old. Not eighty. Laura's gran still went out to work every day, as a telephone operator. Laura wouldn't want her gran to die!

"See, when people get old," said Zilla, "they look back and remember all the people that used to be around when they were young … like in Gran's case there's Granddad, and her mum and her dad, and her own gran, and her little brother. They're all *dead*," said Zilla. "So when she dies it means she'll be able to meet them again. And that's got to be nice for her," said Zilla, "hasn't it?"

"I suppose so," said Laura; and she wondered if her gran would like to die so that she could meet Grandpa again. Gran had loved Grandpa, but on the other hand she seemed very happy being a telephone operator and having great giggly get-togethers with her friends (who were also telephone operators) and coming to visit Mum and Dad and Laura. Maybe Gran wasn't old enough yet. Laura certainly hoped so.

"Want to play ball?" said Zilla. "See how many times you can bounce it off the wall without dropping it."

After they'd played ball for a bit they went to play with the garden roller. The garden roller was kept in a shed. It was big and heavy and the two girls could only just manage to drag it out between them.

"I've invented this new game," said Zilla.

"You pull the handle down, like this – " she pulled the handle right down as far as the ground – "and then you have to jump over it, quick, before it springs up again."

Zilla was an expert at jumping; she beat the handle every time. Laura wasn't so nimble: after only a few goes she got quite badly clonked.

"Don't tell Mum," urged Zilla, as she dragged Laura into the garden shed to sit on a flower pot and nurse her bruises. "I'm not supposed to play with the roller … p'raps if I gave you a Chinese burn it'd take your mind off it."

Before Laura knew what she was about, Zilla had seized her right arm and was squeezing and rubbing at her wrist with both hands until she was forced to give a yelp of pain.

"But it took your mind off the other, though," said Zilla, "didn't it?"

Laura wasn't at all sure it had: she now

had a sore wrist as well as a whopping great bruise on her left leg.

"You've got to admit," said Zilla.

It would be rude to make a fuss when you were someone's guest. After all, Zilla had only been trying to entertain her. Laura bit hard on her lip. She thought that jumping over rollers was the sort of game that Em would enjoy.

"What shall we do now?" said Zilla.

Laura would have liked to say "Go through the archway and play in the sandpit?" but perhaps it wasn't quite her place to suggest it, and in any case Zilla might think it childish.

"Let's stay here and talk." Zilla dragged up a second flower pot and perched herself companionably on it next to Laura. "What school are you going to go to?"

"St Mary's High."

Zilla nodded. "That's the one I'd go to if we came to live here."

Feeling suddenly brave — Zilla's resemblance to Em was really quite reassuring — Laura said, "Might you come to live here?"

"If Gran dies, we might. I want to, and Mum wants to. So does Dad. The others don't."

Laura pricked up her ears.

"Who are the others?"

"My brother and sister. They're just stick-in-the-muds. Don't want to change schools. At least, that's what they *say*. I reckon they're just scared of the ghost."

"Is there really a ghost?" said Laura, sidetracked.

"Yes, but I'm not allowed to tell you about it."

"Why not?"

"In case it frightens you."

Laura couldn't say that she wouldn't be frightened because the truth was she probably would. Instead she said, "Aren't you frightened?"

"I've never seen it," said Zilla. "My dad did once, when he was a boy. And my gran has, of course; lots of times. It's a very old house. It's even older than my gran."

"Yes, I know," said Laura. "So's ours."

"But yours hasn't got a ghost. At least," said Zilla, "I shouldn't think it has. Ours has had one ever since my gran was a little girl. See, she used to live here when she was young, only there wasn't any ghost right at the beginning 'cos the house wasn't old enough. It's only old houses have ghosts. And the only reason they have them is if something horrible has happened."

Laura waited, breathlessly. She couldn't bring herself to ask if something horrible *had* happened.

"Something really tragic," said Zilla. "Something – " She stopped.

"What?" whispered Laura.

"I can't tell you. I'll get into trouble. It'll give you nightmares. Your mum," said

Zilla, "said you were easily upset."

Laura's cheeks flushed deep scarlet. She felt betrayed. Her mum had been talking about her to strangers! Telling them how she imagined things and couldn't sleep. Zilla must think she was completely loopy.

"I don't have nightmares," said Laura. She thought a lot about death, but she didn't have nightmares.

"I still can't tell you. Mum said I wasn't to talk about it." Zilla jumped up from her flower pot. "Let's put the roller back and see if tea's ready."

As they heaved the roller back, Laura said, "Do your brother and sister ever come to stay here?"

Zilla pulled a face.

"Yes. *Unfortunately*. I like it better without them. You're lucky, being an only child … you don't have anyone to boss you."

Laura wanted to ask whether it was Em

who bossed, but she had promised Mum not to talk about Tommy and Em. It suddenly struck her – here was Zilla's mum telling Zilla not to talk about the ghost, and Laura's mum telling Laura not to talk about the two children (who must be Zilla's brother and sister, which meant that she *hadn't* imagined them). It was a wonder they had found anything to converse about at all.

"Tea should be ready in a minute," said Zilla. "Can you do G-talk?"

Shyly, Laura shook her head. She didn't know what G-talk was.

"It's easy," said Zilla. "I'll teach you … g-can g-you g-do g-G g-talk?"

Zilla rattled it off like a machine gun.

"Now you have a go. G-can g-you g-do g-G g-talk?"

"G-no – g-I – g-can't!" said Laura.

"G-but g-now g-you g-can!"

"G-but – g-only – g-very g-slowly," said Laura.

"G-it'll g-come," said Zilla.

Because of the G-talk, which they practised all through tea, to the despair of Zilla's mum, Laura managed a crumbly slice of cake and two squidgy buns almost without noticing. They ate in the kitchen, which meant there wasn't any tablecloth to worry about, and there wasn't any carpet to drop things on, so that it probably wouldn't have mattered if she had made a mess, but it was nicer that she hadn't. It was Zilla, in her enthusiasm for G-talk, who sprayed crumbs everywhere and knocked over a glass of orange.

"As you will observe, Laura," said Zilla's mum, "this is not exactly what you would call gracious living."

It might not have been gracious living, but it was *comfortable*, thought Laura. The only thing which troubled her slightly was the thought of Zilla's gran. She couldn't help wondering where she was – upstairs?

In her bedroom? – and whether she would mind a strange child coming in to have tea while she was dying.

Laura wasn't at all sure it was right. She was also terrified in case Zilla's mum wanted her to go and say hallo. Grown-ups were always wanting children to go and say hallo to people – mostly old people. Laura had once been taken to a dreadful place where there had been nothing *but* old people, all sitting about in chairs, doing nothing, and to her horror her mum made her go and kiss one of them.

"That was your great gran," she had said, afterwards.

Laura had only been four at the time, but it had frightened her. It wouldn't have frightened Zilla. Zilla was bold, like Em.

"G-you g-must g-come g-again," she said, as Laura left.

"Oh, Zilla! Do speak English," said her mum. "I can't understand a word you say."

"G-Laura g-can," said Zilla.
She giggled; so did Laura.

Chapter Three

All over the weekend it rained again –
and Laura's tonsils came back. Not
quite as badly as before, but bad enough to
make her mum shake her head, and sigh,
and say that sooner or later they would have
to be taken out.

"But I need them!" wailed Laura. "We
wouldn't have been given tonsils if we
didn't need them!"

"You certainly don't need them if
they're going to keep on getting
infected," said her mum. "You'll be

far better off without them."

Laura lay on the sofa and worried. How did they take tonsils out? Did they have to cut your throat open? Or did they put a pair of long scissors down you and snip?

She was still worrying on Monday morning, when Zilla came round.

"G-hi!" said Zilla, bouncing across to the sofa as if on springs. "G-I g-came g-to g-see g-if g-you – "

"I think I'd better leave you two together," said Laura's mum. "I'll be upstairs if you need me."

"I came to see if you wanted to come up the park," said Zilla, "but your mum says you've got tonsillitis."

Laura nodded, self-pityingly. "I keep getting it."

"Horrid!" said Zilla. "I used to till I had my tonsils out."

"You've had them out?" Laura sat up and stared at Zilla's throat, searching for scars.

There didn't seem to be any. "Did they cut you open?"

"Don't know what they did." Zilla gave one of her Em-type cackles. "I didn't stay awake long enough to find out!"

"Did it hurt?" said Laura.

"Only a bit. Not as bad as when I cut my knee open. You ought to have yours out," said Zilla, "then you wouldn't keep getting ill."

"I don't want them out! I don't like the thought of an operation."

"Pooh! Operation's nothing," said Zilla. "I've had two. Once for tonsils, and once when I fell off my sister's bike and smashed my head. They thought I might have brain damage. My sister says I have."

The way Zilla spoke, she made it sound as if operations were something to boast about. Almost something to enjoy. Laura looked at her, dubiously.

"Did you have to stay in hospital?"

"You bet!" said Zilla.

Laura had never been in hospital (except for when she was born, and she couldn't remember that). She had never even visited any. She imagined them as being full of beds, nothing but beds, with rows and rows of people all bloody and operated on, lying there groaning.

"Hospital's fun," said Zilla. "I met my best friend in hospital ... well, she used to be my best friend. She isn't any more 'cos we quarrelled and now I hate her and she won't talk to me. But before we quarrelled she was my best friend. We had our tonsils out together. It was great! 'Cos afterwards you can't eat properly so you get to have all nice stuff like jelly and ice cream. And people keep visiting you and bringing you prezzies. And everyone sends you cards and things. Also you get off school," she added.

Laura perked up. "Don't you like school?"

Laura didn't very much, herself. She didn't mind the lessons, it was all the other children that bothered her.

"Oh, school's OK, I suppose." Zilla perched on the arm of the sofa and began picking at one of the cushions. "Sometimes. When you've got a best friend."

Laura had never had a best friend. At Turpin Street Juniors she had teamed up with a girl called Olive Mounsey, but that had only been because Olive Mounsey was too unpopular to go round with anyone else. They hadn't even been friends, let alone best friends. The only sort of best friends Laura had ever come close to making were the people she met in books.

"What I'm *not* looking forward to," said Zilla, "is next term. I've got to go to this really gross school called Park Hill Rise which is top of the league for bullying. They've got worse bullies at Park Hill Rise than anywhere, almost. My best friend that *used* to be my best friend knew someone that went there that ran away, she was bullied so much. They've got these gangs of big kids, see, that pick on you."

Laura shook her head, sympathetically. It was a comfort to know that even Zilla had *some* things she was scared of.

"What about your sister?" said Laura. Em must obviously be a bit older than Zilla. "Won't she protect you?"

"Her?" Zilla trumpeted, derisively. "She wouldn't even cross the playground! Last term when someone beat me up she said it was my fault. She said I asked for it, being cocky. She's so *superior*, my sister. Thinks she's so *clever*."

"What about – " Laura was on the point of saying, "What about Tommy?" when she remembered, just in time, what she had promised her mum. "What about your brother?" she said.

"Him? He's just a womble!"

Laura didn't like to ask what a womble was. It was obviously something that Zilla held in contempt. Poor Tommy! He was still only a baby. She wondered if he minded, being away from his mum all this time. She couldn't help feeling that Zilla was being a bit hard on him, though she could see that Zilla and Em might possibly not get on. They were too alike.

"You're ever so lucky," said Zilla, "going to St Mary's. St Mary's is a really nice school. I wish I could go there."

Laura wished she could, as well. It would make all the difference, starting at a new school, if she could start there with Zilla.

She didn't like to say, "Maybe if your gran dies you'll be able to," but Zilla said it for her.

"If Gran dies before next term we might give up our house and move here and then we could both go to St Mary's together. That'd be good, wouldn't it? You and me together? It's just my horrible brother and sister, that's all. 'Cos *they* don't want to move. They say I'm a snob 'cos all we've got's a council house and that's why I want to come here, but it's not that at all. It's Park Hill Rise. I know some of the kids that go there, and they've really got it in for me. I tell you," said Zilla, "having your tonsils out is nothing compared – " she switched hastily to G-talk as Laura's mum came back – "g-with g-going g-to g-Park g-Hill g-Rise!"

"You and Zilla seem to be getting on well," said Laura's mum, when Zilla had gone zooming off to the park by herself. "When you're feeling up to it, we'll ask her round to tea, shall we?"

"Yes, I'd like that," said Laura.

*   *   *

Next day Laura's tonsils had almost gone, but her mum said she was to stay indoors until her temperature was back to normal.

"I'm just going to pop out and do a bit of shopping. I won't be long. You can have the television on if you want."

Laura didn't feel like watching television any more. She took her book about the olden times and curled up on the window seat beneath the big sash windows which looked out on to the front garden.

Olden times people, when you got down to it, were really not very much different from people of today, but they did have a terrible tendency to use complicated language and talk in sentences that went on for ever. Before very long, Laura found her eyelids drooping and her chin falling forward on to her chest.

Of course it wasn't just the book; it was the tonsils as well. She was usually very good at reading difficult books. Mrs Bell, at Turpin Road, had said she was one of the most advanced readers she had ever had. It was the olden times talk and the tonsils both coming together which had defeated her. She really ought to have chosen an easier sort of book, but she had read the whole of Roald Dahl, and the whole of Judy Blume, and she had grown out of Enid Blyton, and the *Lord of the Rings* was too long, and she hadn't yet joined the local library, and …

Zzzz! went Laura, snoring gently to herself.

She was woken by the sound of the front gate opening. It must be Mum, come home from shopping.

Laura sat up and pushed her hair out of her eyes. She looked at the clock. It couldn't be Mum! She had only been gone ten minutes.

Cautiously, she peeped out through the window. A girl with red hair was coming up the path. It was Kate! Whatever could she want? Zilla wouldn't have sent her; Kate was a friend of Em, not of Zilla. Laura bet

Zilla didn't like any of Em's friends, just like Em probably didn't like any of Zilla's. There had been two girls at Turpin Road who had been sisters and who had hated each other. Laura's mum had always said that it just went to show ... "Even if you did have a sister you wouldn't necessarily like her."

Laura sat and waited for the doorbell to ring. (Number 44 didn't have a black tongue knocker like number 42. Laura's dad had fitted up a proper electric bell.) She waited and waited, but nothing happened. What was Kate up to?

Secreting herself behind one of the thick red curtains (donated by Gran), Laura peered out into the garden. Kate was nowhere to be seen! She must have gone back out again. Perhaps she had meant to go next door and had come to the wrong house by mistake. That was probably what it was.

Laura picked up her book and did her best to concentrate. She wasn't going to be beaten: Laura always finished a book once she had started it.

She had just worked her way to the end of a really long, involved sentence all full of dashes and things in brackets, when the doorbell rang and made her jump. Laura laid down her book. She wasn't supposed to answer the door if her mum wasn't there. But if it was only Kate – Kate come back again …

Maybe Zilla and her mum were out and Kate wanted to leave a message for them. A message for Zilla to give to Em.

Laura slid off the window seat and went out into the hall. The front door had stained glass panels and she could see someone standing on the other side of it but she couldn't tell whether it was Kate or not. It looked as if it could be. It was someone not very tall.

Laura opened the door just a crack, keeping the chain on. An old lady stood there. A small old lady with snow-white hair.

"Oh!" she said. "I am so sorry, my dear. I thought the house was still empty. I'm afraid I've been prying. You must forgive me! My grandmother used to live here a long time ago. I couldn't resist, as I was in the area – "

"We've just moved here," said Laura.

"I do apologize! Such terrible manners! My grandmother would be ashamed of me. I ought to have rung at the bell first, instead of snooping about like some intruder. I do hope I didn't frighten you?"

"Not at all," said Laura, politely.

"Good. I shouldn't like to think that I had done that. Is your mummy at home by any chance?"

"Mum's out," said Laura. "She's gone shopping." And then, remembering that you should never tell strangers that you were on your own: "She'll be back any minute," she added.

"I was wondering if I might possibly come in and have a look at the old place. I'll tell you what I'll do, I'll go and call next door first and try again in about half an hour. If your mummy comes back, will you tell her?"

"All right," said Laura.

"Thank you so much. My name is Armitage, by the way. Miss Armitage. Tell your mummy I'm an old friend of Mrs Hobbs, next door ... old Mrs Hobbs, that is."

When Mum came in with the shopping, Laura said, "A lady called. Her name's Miss Armitage. She's an old friend of Mrs Hobbs next door. *Old* Mrs Hobbs. And her grandmother used to live here and she's coming back in half an hour."

"You mean, you opened the door to her?" said her mum.

"Yes, because I thought she was – " Laura stopped and bit her tongue. She couldn't say she thought Miss Armitage was Kate. Laura's mum didn't know about Kate. "I thought she was Zilla," said Laura.

"Why? You're not expecting Zilla, are you?"

"I thought I – I thought I saw Zilla. In the garden." Laura's mum looked at her, sharply.

"Laura, I've told you before," she said, "don't answer the door to *anybody*. Not unless you're absolutely certain."

"I left the chain on," said Laura.

"Well, that's better than nothing, but I'd rather you didn't open the door at all. What does this Miss Armitage want, anyway?"

"She wants to look round the house."

"What, now?" cried Laura's mum. "Look at the state of it! Is your bed made?"

"Yes," said Laura.

"Well, mine isn't! Go and see to it for

me, quickly, while I put this shopping away."

Miss Armitage rang the bell while Laura was still shaking up Mum and Dad's duvet. Laura stood listening, at the head of the stairs. She heard Mum asking Miss Armitage to come in, and Miss Armitage apologizing all over again for snooping, and saying how her grandmother used to live here many years ago, and Mum saying why not come through to the kitchen and have a cup of coffee.

"Laura!" her mum called to her, up the stairs. "Do you want a drink of something?"

Laura arrived in the kitchen in time to hear Miss Armitage telling Mum about her grandmother.

"Oh! A real holy terror, she was. Spare the rod and spoil the child, that was her motto. I used to come and stay with her sometimes, in my school holidays. I got on with her all right, but oh, dear! All the neighbourhood children went in fear of their lives. You've heard of Betsy Trotwood, have you?" She swung round on Laura, who shyly shook her head. "Betsy Trotwood, from *David Copperfield*? David's Aunt Betsy? Now, that *is* a good book! You should read that. I'd read it at least twice by the time I was your age. Do you like reading?"

"Yes, she loves it," said Laura's mum.

"That's excellent! You'll never be alone so long as you've got a good book. Children don't read nearly enough these days. Fancy never having heard of Betsy Trotwood! Too much television. Too many computer games."

Laura's mum winked at her across the old lady's head.

"If there was one thing," said Miss Armitage, "that Betsy Trotwood couldn't stand it was donkeys being ridden across her grass verge. She used to keep watch behind the curtains and every time she saw one she'd cry, 'Janet! Donkeys!' and Janet would have to go running out there with a stick and get rid of them. Janet was the servant, do you see."

"I see." Laura said it gravely. She wasn't quite sure what Miss Armitage was talking about, but it sounded interesting. Laura liked donkeys.

"Well, now," said Miss Armitage, settling down with her coffee, "my grandmother didn't have servants, though she did have all her groceries delivered and sent her washing to the laundry, but when it came to children running up and down the street she was just the same as Betsy Trotwood. 'Clear off!' she used to shout. 'You clear off!' She didn't really care for children; only me. She made an exception for me because I was her granddaughter. Oh, I used to enjoy coming to stay! Such games we used to have, the Hobbs children and I. I remember, in the summer ... "

Laura sat at the table, nibbling biscuits and sipping at her orange juice while Miss Armitage told them how it had been in the days of her youth. Laura didn't know how old Miss Armitage was, but she thought that her youth must have been a very long time ago.

"Of course I was born in 1917," said Miss Armitage, as if reading Laura's thoughts. She looked sternly at Laura over the rim of her coffee cup. "Do you know what was happening in 1917, young lady?"

Laura's cheeks flushed, anxiously. She didn't know anything had happened in 1917 (apart from Miss Armitage being born).

"There was a war on," said Miss Armitage. "The Great War. Don't you do history at school these days?"

"She's only just left juniors," said Laura's mum. "She hasn't yet started at the big school."

"Like that Zilla next door. She didn't know, either. I came principally to visit my old friend, do you see. Mrs Hobbs. I fear she is very poorly. She cannot have long to go."

Hastily, Laura's mum pushed her chair back.

"Would you like to see upstairs now you're here?"

"I won't go upstairs, thank you all the same. My legs are not what they were. You'll discover, when you're older – " Miss Armitage nodded again at Laura – "you'll find you're full of aches and pains you never even thought about when you were young. I walked up the stairs next door and my knees have been protesting ever since. You'll hear them, as I get up."

Slowly, Miss Armitage levered herself upright. Laura listened with interest to hear the knees but they didn't even crack (which Laura's sometimes did).

"Something I should like to see," said Miss Armitage, "is the garden, if I may."

"Of course." Laura's mum led the way across the kitchen.

"Many a happy hour have I spent out here ... such sport we used to have!"

"I'm afraid you'll find it's been rather let go. We're meaning to do some work on it but so far we just haven't had a chance."

"And you're not gardeners," said Laura.

"No! And we're not gardeners. But at least we'll clear the ground ivy."

"And the brambles," said Laura.

"Yes, *they* certainly weren't here in my time. My grandmother used to have the most beautiful flower beds. Over there. By the escallonia." Miss Armitage pointed, with the umbrella, towards the pink bush. "Oh, dear! How cross she used to get if my ball went anywhere near them. 'Child,' she used to cry, 'you keep away from my flower beds!' She always called me child," said

Miss Armitage, "although she was quite fond of me."

Laura thought that it was a good thing her dad wasn't here. Her mum had far more patience than her dad. Dad would have gone stomping off ages ago muttering about "tiresome old women".

Miss Armitage did ramble rather, though Laura didn't find her tiresome. She thought it was interesting, hearing about the olden times from a real olden times person.

"I'm reading a book," she said, eagerly, "about a girl who was born in the reign of Queen Victoria."

"*What Katy Did*," said Miss Armitage. "That's a good book."

Laura opened her mouth to say that it wasn't *What Katy Did* (*What Katy Did* was easy: she had read that when she was only nine), but already Miss Armitage had moved on to something else.

"What, pray – " she pointed again, in a

different direction this time, with her umbrella – "what are those monstrosities?"

"Fir trees?" said Laura's mum.

"Leyland cypresses. Dreadful things! Grow like weeds. *They* were not here in my grandmother's time."

"They do make quite an effective screen," pleaded Laura's mum. "That road out the back is a race track."

"It never used to be so," said Miss Armitage. "I can remember when that road was a footpath. I remember the year they came with their bulldozers. Bulldozed all across the fields and built on them. Turned the footpath into a motorway. Well, it wasn't a motorway in those days, of course. But quite busy enough. The noise was appalling. And the accidents."

There was a pause.

"That's why we don't have a cat," said Laura's mum. Laura had been agitating for a cat, now that they had a proper house and garden. "It would be over that wall at the bottom before you could say knife. And that would be that – squashed cat."

"Never mind cats," said Miss Armitage. "I could tell you something far worse than cats."

"Yes. Well –" Mum had turned away and was plucking the heads off some dead-looking flowers. "I've promised her another guinea-pig, instead. At least guinea-pigs don't roam."

"Unlike children," said Miss Armitage.

"Look! I don't know what these are," said Mum, brightly.

"Weeds." Miss Armitage spared them scarcely a glance. "When I was a girl there were back gates leading on to that road – not that it was a road, when I first used to come here. It only became a road when I was about your age." She looked down at Laura. "What age are you?"

"Eleven," said Laura.

"Eleven? I thought you were older than that. You young people grow up too fast these days. I was fourteen; I was still a child. I played with my dolls. Do you play with your dolls?"

Laura shook her head.

"You see? It's as I said: you grow up too fast. I blame the television. We had no such thing when I was young. And far better for it!"

"Laura watches very little television," said Laura's mum.

"But she doesn't play with her dolls. Thinks herself too sophisticated, no doubt."

"Oh, I wouldn't say so." Laura's mum rushed to her defence. "I wouldn't call Laura at all sophisticated. She's quite sensible for her age, but she's still very much a child."

"Hm!" Miss Armitage sniffed, plainly not believing a word of it. "This generation don't know what childhood is. When I was fourteen I was totally innocent. Totally shielded from the facts of life. That is, until they started bulldozing the fields and turning the footpath into a road. That was when I grew up, very suddenly."

Miss Armitage lapsed for a moment into silence. Laura and her mum stood, politely waiting.

"They turned the footpath into a road, do you see; a road for traffic. It was the end of civilization as we knew it. Bicycles, delivery vans, young tearaways in goggles roaring along at ninety miles per hour. It was not what we were used to. We were used to running straight out into the fields. All along Hindes Road, from where the flats are at the top down as far as the entrance to the park, we all had back gates leading out there. You probably still have yours, behind those ghastly trees. What an eyesore! My grandmother would turn in her grave. They haven't next door, of course. No back gate there. They got rid of theirs smart enough. Too late, unfortunately."

Laura was about to protest that they hadn't got rid of it, it was still there, she had seen it, when her mum and Miss Armitage both began to talk at once.

"Everything must have changed so much," said Mum.

"It was in all the papers," said Miss Armitage.

"Horse-drawn vehicles – "

"The most tragic accident, they called it."

"Steam trains – "

"Of course, the family never really got over it."

Never got over what? thought Laura. She would have liked to ask, but already Mum was shepherding Miss Armitage back up the garden towards the house.

Miss Armitage didn't stay long after that. She stood for a few minutes in the kitchen telling them about the bells that had been rung for the servants, when people had had any servants, and she looked into the front room and wondered what had happened to the fireplace and the wooden shutters that had been at the windows, and then, to Mum's relief – Laura could see that by now even Mum had had enough – she said that she really must be going.

"Do you think we *have* got a gate at the bottom of the garden?" said Laura, when the front door had finally closed on Miss Armitage.

"I don't know," said Mum. "Let's go and have a look."

They found the gate, behind the fir trees (Leyland cypresses, Miss Armitage had called them). It obviously hadn't been used for a great many years. Laura tried tugging at it but the hinges groaned in protest and it opened just a little way, hardly wide enough even for someone as small as Laura to squeeze through.

"All the same," said Laura's mum, "I think we'll get Dad to board it up. That's a very nasty road out there."

That evening, before tea, because the sun was out and the tonsils seemed to be on the mend again, Laura was doing some skipping in the garden when there was a shout from the other side and a head appeared over the fence. She thought at first that it was Em, but it wasn't. It was Zilla.

"G-hi!" called Zilla. "G-are g-you g-alone?"

The speed at which Zilla spoke G-talk was really amazing. She made it sound like a foreign language.

"G-yes, g-my g-mum g-is g-g – " Laura stumbled, as she nearly always did. She couldn't wrap her tongue round the words anywhere near as fast as Zilla. "She's in the kitchen," said Laura, "getting my dad's tea."

"Good." Zilla hung there, with just her hands and her head visible. "I'm standing on a bucket. I think it might give way any minute. Did an old woman come to see you?"

"Yes," said Laura. "Did she come and see you?"

"She came to see my gran. They used to play together when they were girls."

"She was telling us about when she was a girl," said Laura. "How they bulldozed the fields and it was the end of civilization."

"She's incredibly old," said Zilla. "Almost as old as my gran."

"She grew up very suddenly," said Laura, "when they turned the footpath into a road."

"I know all about that," said Zilla.

"What? About them turning the footpath into a road?"

"About her growing up suddenly."

"Why did she?" said Laura.

"Because – "

Zilla stopped.

"Because what?" said Laura.

"I can't tell you!"

Laura moved closer to the snatching brambles. "Why not?"

"Give you nightmares."

"I don't have nightmares!"

"You would if I told you."

"Why?"

"'Cos it's gruesome!"

"Is it – " Laura hesitated – "is it to do with the ghost?"

"Can't tell you! I'll get you into trouble if I t– aaaaaaaaaaargh!"

With a loud screech, Zilla suddenly disappeared. Laura heard a bang and a thud, followed by the sound of swearing.

"Aow! Blast! Ouch!"

"Are you all right?" said Laura.

"My foot's gone through the bucket!"

"Won't it come out again?"

"No!" Zilla giggled. "Listen! Can you hear me?" Clank, clank, clank went Zilla.

"Yes," said Laura. "What are you doing?"

"G-I'm g-walking g-around," sang Zilla, "g-with g-my g-foot g-in g-a g-bucket ... g-in g-a g-bucket!"

"G-in g-a g-bucket!" sang Laura.

She still couldn't do G-talk as well as Zilla but she was getting better.

Chapter Four

One evening after work, Laura's dad went out to make a start on clearing the garden.

"No use to keep on putting it off," he said. "Got to get to grips with it sooner or later."

Laura's mum wanted him to start on the ground ivy ("Horrible stuff, all over the place!") but Laura begged for the brambles.

"Please, Dad! They're choking the escallonia."

"The what?" said her dad.

"The escallonia," said Laura. "The poor pink bush... it's being *strangled*."

"Dear, dear! Can't have that," said her dad. "Can't strangle an esca – how did it go again?"

"Escallonia," said Laura.

"Can't strangle an escallonia."

Her dad fetched the new garden shears, and the new garden fork and spade, and Laura put on her mum's new gardening gloves and trundled out the new wheelbarrow, and pretty soon the brambles were being hacked and slashed and torn up by the roots. Laura found that in spite of their being so snatchy and scratchy she didn't actually enjoy destroying them, but it was their own fault: they shouldn't have tried to crowd out the escallonia. It was just another form of bullying, because the brambles had prickles and the escallonia didn't.

"There used to be a flower bed here

once," said Laura, jogging back with the wheelbarrow from the new compost heap they were making at the bottom of the garden, behind the fir trees. (The Leyland cypresses: she wanted to get their names right.) "That was in Miss Armitage's day. A lovely flower bed."

"Oh, yes?" said her dad.

"And the back gate used to open out on to *fields*."

"I'll buy a padlock for that gate … I don't want you running out there. Ridiculous arrangement," grumbled her dad. "Main road right outside the back gate."

"The gate doesn't open properly anyway," said Laura.

"No, but I'd rather be on the safe side." Her dad straightened up and wiped the back of his hand across his brow. "Accidents have been known … pass me that fork, will you? This one's a tough little so-and-so."

It took Laura and her dad most of the

evening to clear the brambles away from the pink bush. Laura kept hoping that Tommy's Rollsy would come to light, but all they found were an old glass bottle and half a china plate, which Dad said they would take indoors to show Mum.

"Willow pattern, that is, same as my old nan used to have."

"It's pretty," said Laura; but what she really wanted was Tommy's Rollsy. She was sure this was the spot where it had landed. Poor Em must have been scratched to pieces, crawling about in all those brambles.

"That's the good thing about a Victorian garden," said her dad, as they put the wheelbarrow and the garden tools away. "You never know what you might turn up. This bottle, for instance ... see the glass? Not like modern glass, is it? See all the flaws in it?"

Laura nodded, dutifully. The glass was green and the bottle was tiny, almost a miniature. At any other time she would have been delighted with it and taken it away to put on her mantelpiece, but just at the moment she was trying to puzzle out the mystery of Rollsy. She *knew* it had fallen into the brambles: she had *seen* it.

"I reckon this is last century," said her dad. "Late last century or early this. Might be people who'd pay money for this sort of thing. You ought to have a bit of a dig around tomorrow and see if you can unearth some more."

"All right," said Laura. She might unearth Rollsy at the same time.

* * *

Next day it rained yet again. Laura had never known a summer so wet; rain was such a *nuisance*. Even so she would have put on her anorak and gone out to dig, but in the morning her mum wouldn't let her – "Don't be so ridiculous! It's coming down in buckets! You'll get soaked through" – and in the afternoon she couldn't because Zilla was coming to tea. Her mum had made banana sandwiches and coconut pyramids and said that if they wanted they could take them up to Laura's room and have a picnic.

"G-shall g-we?" said Zilla.

"G-why g-not?" said Laura's mum. "Oh!" She clapped a hand to her mouth. "I'm sorry! I'm not supposed to know the language, am I? It's all right, I only understand a few words."

Zilla grinned. "G-it's g-not g-for g-adults," she said.

"Quite right," said Laura's mum. "Off you go, then! I'll bring your tea up to you in a little while."

This time last week Laura would have been petrified at the thought of being left on her own to entertain Zilla in her bedroom, but she had learnt by now that

Zilla wasn't someone who needed entertaining: she entertained herself.

"What's this?" she kept saying, as she picked things up from Laura's mantelpiece or from the shelves that Laura's dad had fitted by the side of her bed.

"That's my Wade," said Laura. She had over thirty pieces of Wade pottery. She had been collecting it since she was eight years old and always asked for it at Christmas and birthdays.

"What's this?"

"That's a jug I made at Juniors ... that's a Spanish doll my gran brought back from holiday ... that's a special candle that smells like apples ... that's a Victorian bottle we found in the garden."

"It's so *sweet*," crooned Zilla, holding the bottle up to the light.

Laura wished she could say that Zilla could have it, but her dad wanted her to find more so that he could sell them.

"I'm going to dig again tomorrow," said Laura, "if it's dry. We've pulled all the brambles up and I'm going to make a flower bed. I might f–" She was going to say, "I might find Tommy's Rollsy." It was so difficult, remembering all the time that she wasn't supposed to mention Tommy or Em. Surely Mum wouldn't mind her mentioning them *now*? Now that Zilla knew she wasn't mad? "I might find your brother's Rollsy," she said, but already Zilla had set down the bottle and gone flickering off across the room to pick up something else and didn't hear her.

"What's this?"

"That's my World Wildlife money box," said Laura. "When you put money in it, it makes jungle noises."

"Oh! I haven't got any money!" wailed Zilla. "Let's put something in, I want to hear it!"

Laura took the top off the money box and

tipped out the money, and watched while Zilla happily put it all back in again, listening to the jungle sounds.

"That is *brilliant*," said Zilla. "Oh, you are so lucky having this room to yourself! I have to share with my sister. I hate her. She's coming to stay with us this weekend, worse luck. *And* my brother. It's been really nice without them."

"Don't you like them at all?" said Laura.

"No. I hate them. They pick on me – well, *she* does, my sister. My brother's just incredibly boring. He's the most boring person I've ever known. My gran sleeps in this room," said Zilla.

"Which room?" Laura looked at her, bewildered. Zilla had a habit of leaping from one subject to another so fast that sometimes Laura couldn't keep up.

"This one." Zilla flung her arms wide, indicating Laura's bedroom. "Her bed's just there," she pointed to the fireplace, "only on the other side of the room. Like yours is. Imagine," said Zilla, "if there was a door you could walk right through!"

It was the last thing Laura wanted to imagine. She found it rather scary to think that on the other side of her bedroom wall an old lady lay dying. She wished Zilla hadn't told her.

"There!" said Zilla. "You've gone all white! Just 'cos I said my gran sleeps in the same bedroom as you … you'd *freak* if I told you about the ghost!"

"No, I wouldn't," said Laura.

"Yes, you would! You'd freak."

"Try me," said Laura.

"No. You'd only go and faint or something and then I'd get into a row."

Laura was indignant: she had never fainted in her life!

"What d'you want to know for, anyway? You wouldn't see the ghost. My gran's the only one that sees the ghost."

"I thought you said your dad had?"

"Only once. And that was when he was a little boy, same age as – "

"As who?"

"Not telling!" Zilla threw up the sash window and leaned out. "I bet if I was a burglar I could swarm right up that drainpipe."

"Yes, and swarm right down it again, head first!" said Laura's mum, coming in with a tray full of banana sandwiches and coconut pyramids. "You get yourself back in and have your tea."

When Zilla left, she said, "I won't be able to see you tomorrow or Sunday 'cos my dad's going to be here. But I'll come round on Monday, shall I? Or you could come round to me. You come and have tea with me, then I'll come round and have tea with you. That's the best way. Then it's fair."

"All right," said Laura.

On Saturday the sun came out and Laura spent all morning digging with a small hand trowel where the brambles had been. It would have been quicker with a spade, but the spade was too heavy for her. Fortunately the earth was soft after all the rain, but it was still hard work and the sun on her bare head made her feel quite sleepy, so that every now and again she had to stop digging and crawl into the shade to rest.

It was during one of her resting periods that she heard Em's voice at the far end of the garden. She knew it was Em's; she had learnt, by now, to tell it apart from Zilla's. They were very alike, but Em's voice was louder and deeper. At the moment it was *very* loud. She seemed to be shouting at someone. Her voice rose and fell and then rang out, quite piercingly. She must be in a simply terrific rage. Laura hoped it wasn't Tommy she was yelling at.

After a bit, as the noise went on, Laura

crawled out from under her apple tree and crept up the path to sneak a look. She would just peep over the fence and check that Em wasn't doing anything terrible, like beating poor Tommy to a pulp.

Cautiously, Laura scrambled up the timber pile and peered over the broken fence into next-door's garden. To her surprise, Em was on her own. She was standing near the sandpit, frantically waving her arms and shouting, with what looked like a red bath towel pinned to her shoulders and a big leather belt buckled round her waist with a wooden sword pushed through it.

"*Once more unto the breach, dear friends, once more!*" bawled Em, hurling herself forward into the sandpit. "*Or close the wall up with our English DEAD. In PEACE,*" shrieked Em, planting both legs in the sandpit and brandishing a fist above her head, "*there's nothing so BECOMES a man as modest stillness and humility. BUT,*" bellowed Em, charging up and out of the pit, "*when the blast of WAR blows in our ears, THEN imitate the action of the TIGER –* graaaaaaaaaaargh!" roared Em, making straight for Laura and the fence.

It was too late to crouch down: Em must have seen her. Laura stood helpless as Em's face, contorted with tigerish fury, came to a full stop directly beneath her.

There was a pause. Laura opened her mouth.

"I'm sorry," whispered Laura. "I didn't mean to spy."

"*Stiffen the sinews!*" snarled Em, waving a clenched fist in Laura's direction. "*Summon up the blood!*" Em breathed, deeply, through her nostrils. "*Then lend the eye*" (her eyeballs rolled in their sockets) "*a terrible aspect –* "

The performance went on. Em was obviously so engrossed in what she was doing that she didn't notice Laura standing there, even though Laura was in full view. Laura held her breath and didn't dare to move. She supposed it must be Shakespeare. Laura didn't know much about Shakespeare except that he wrote plays you had to study when you were older. Em, in fact, actually looked older than Laura remembered, maybe because she was acting, and because she was wearing a sweater and skirt – and of course a red towel – instead of a flowery dress.

"*The game's afoot!*" hollered Em. "*Follow your spirit, and on this charge, cry God for HARRY, ENGLAND, and SAINT GEOOOOORGE ...*"

Em's voice disappeared, whooping, up the garden, as Em did a brisk about-turn, and went cantering off through the archway, summoning her troops with her. For one moment Laura half expected to see throngs of men, and horses, and knights in armour. Zilla hadn't told her that Em was an actress.

If that was Shakespeare, thought Laura, then maybe he wasn't so bad.

Laura went back to her digging. By lunch time she had managed to unearth two pieces of china (both broken), an old and rusty tin, half a house brick and a small blue bottle, but no Rollsy. She took the bottle in to her dad, who washed it under the tap and said, "That's a Victorian medicine bottle, that is."

"Can you sell it?" said Laura.

"Might be able to. There's some folk collect these things."

Laura wouldn't have minded collecting them herself, but she knew her mum and dad needed the money. When they had lived in the flat near King's Cross they had only had to pay rent, but now they were living in a proper house they had to pay a mortgage, and this was something which worried them. Laura knew it worried them because whenever they discussed the possibility of going somewhere or buying something one of them would always say, "Think of the mortgage!" And then they would decide that they couldn't afford to go wherever it was or buy what they had wanted.

Laura felt secretly rather guilty, because the only reason her mum and dad had moved from the flat was because of Laura and the non-existent baby that kept crying in the night. If it hadn't been for Laura, they wouldn't have to keep thinking of the mortgage.

"After lunch," said Laura, "if you like, I'll go and look for more."

"Don't tire yourself out," said her mum.

"I'm not tired," said Laura. "I like digging."

By four o'clock she had dug all round where the brambles had been and all she had found were two old coins, one which said "sixpence" and "GVIR 1950" and one which was so old she couldn't read it but which her dad said was a Victorian penny. He ought to be able to sell *that*.

"Are you going to stop and come in now?" said her mum.

"I'll just have a bit of a dig under the escallonia," said Laura.

Her mum shook her head.

"We're not that desperate for cash, you know!"

"No, but it's interesting," said Laura. "It's history."

She had been digging under the escallonia for only a few minutes when her trowel struck something. She didn't think it could be Rollsy, it didn't feel hard enough; more like another piece of broken china.

She sat back on her heels, wondering whether to bother.

"After this," said Laura to herself, "I'm going to give up."

She dug carefully with her trowel, just in

case the hidden object was a bottle. Slowly, she began to uncover it. It wasn't a bottle and it wasn't a piece of china; it was a lump of wood.

At first, disappointed, she was going to throw it away, but then it occurred to her that the wood was an interesting shape, and so she began to brush away the earth which clung to it, and as she brushed she saw that the interesting shape was the shape of a car ...

Excited, she took the trowel and started chipping and scraping. Two large chunks of damp earth fell away, and she found that the car still had wheels. Could it be Rollsy?

"Look!" She ran indoors, into the kitchen, where her mum and dad were having a cup of tea. "Look what I've found!"

"My goodness," said her dad. "That's been there a time and a half." He took it from her. "Hand-carved, I should say ... nice piece of craftsmanship. Let's get it properly cleaned up."

When it was all scrubbed, and dried with one of Mum's tea towels, the car looked almost as good as new except that most of the paint had peeled off.

"Hard wood," said Laura's dad, tapping it against the kitchen table. "Oak, from the feel of it. That's why it's lasted. Look at this!" He showed Laura. "Whoever did it even went to the trouble of carving out the doors and windows."

"Is it a Rolls-Royce?" said Laura.

"Dunno about a Rolls-Royce – though, yes, I suppose it could be. It's certainly quality. None of your assembly-line stuff. This is your actual limo, this is. Must have been some little kid's pride and joy."

"Is it very old, do you think?" said Laura's mum. Laura's dad held it up and squinted at the bottom of it.

"JH, 1924 … that's over seventy years ago."

"A family heirloom!" said Laura. It must have been handed down to Tommy by his dad, who might even have had it from *his* dad. No wonder Tommy had been so upset when Em threw it over the fence. It made Em's crime even worse. Fancy throwing away a family heirloom!

"Could be worth a bob or two." Laura's dad turned the car over in his hands. "I might try ringing up one of the museums … there's one in Bethnal Green specializes in kids' toys. See how much they reckon it's worth."

Laura's face fell. "You're not going to sell it?" she cried.

"Could make a fair bit. There's quite a market for this sort of stuff."

"But, Dad – " It wasn't her dad's to sell! It was Tommy's. "It doesn't belong to us!" said Laura.

"So who do you reckon it belongs to? It was found in our garden, wasn't it?"

"Yes, but it was – it was thrown over from next door. I saw it!"

Laura's mum and dad exchanged glances.

"When did you see it?" said Laura's mum.

"Just a little while ago. When they were playing."

"When who were playing?"

"Zilla's brother and sister."

Her mum frowned. Her dad said, "Whatever you saw being thrown, it certainly wasn't this. This has been there for more than a year or two. Wherever it came from originally, it's ours now. Finders keepers."

"But, Dad – " Laura was almost in tears. After all the trouble she had gone to find it! And it *was* Tommy's Rollsy; it had to be. There couldn't be two Rollsies. All the rain must have washed the paint off and made it look as if it had been there longer than it had.

"Did you want to keep it?" said Laura's mum. She turned to her dad. "She could hang on to it, couldn't she? After all, she was the one who found it – and finders keepers. You just said!"

"What about the bottles? Wouldn't you rather have the bottles?"

Laura shook her head vehemently.

"Cars aren't girls' toys!" said her dad.

"Oh, now, really!" Laura's mum snatched at Rollsy. "That is such a Stone Age remark! Here you are, Laura. You found it, you keep it."

That night, when Laura went to bed, she put the car under her pillow (at the edge, where it wouldn't jab into her head). Tomorrow, if she felt brave, she would take it next door for Tommy.

Chapter Five

Whether it was because of the car tucked under her pillow, or whether it was because she was overtired after all her digging, Laura had a restless night full of strange, sad dreams which kept waking her up.

Every time she woke she found her cheeks wet with tears, even though the dreams had disappeared and she couldn't remember what they had been about. Then she would lie for ages tossing and turning and thinking of Zilla's gran in the bedroom next door, wondering what it must be like to be an old lady and to know that you were dying. This, naturally, made her feel sad all over again, and scared as well, so that then she was *afraid* to go to sleep, and just as afraid of staying awake.

In the old days, when she was little, she would have gone into Mum and Dad's room, and Dad would have gone grumbling into Laura's bed and Laura would have crawled in beside Mum, but you couldn't do that sort of thing when you were eleven. You were supposed to be more grown up. It was very babyish to go creeping in to sleep with your mum.

Laura wrapped the duvet round her head and started to count sheep. Surely by the time she had reached five thousand it would be morning?

She reached as far as three thousand and something and must then have dropped off to sleep again, for when she next woke it was light and there were voices coming from next door's garden. Eagerly she ran to the window and looked out. She couldn't see beyond the trellis, but she could hear the sound of bat hitting ball and Em's voice, jubilant, singing out "Howzatt?"

They must be playing cricket. She wondered if Zilla was out there, and maybe their dad. In books, people's dads always went out into the garden and played cricket with them, and sometimes people's mums, as well.

I could give Tommy his Rollsy, thought Laura.

She wouldn't be shy, she would do it right now, before her dad could change his mind and make her sell it.

As she pulled on her clothes, Laura glanced up at her Swiss cuckoo clock on the wall. It was whirring, which meant the cuckoo was about to pop out at the end of his little spring and start cuckooing. Yes! Here he came.

Cuck-oo, cuck-oo, cuck-oo –

He did it every hour, on the hour; twelve times at midnight and midday.

Cuck-oo, cuck-oo, cuck-oo –

Laura, imagining it must be at least eight o'clock – though even that would be quite early for a Sunday morning – waited for two more, but they never came. The cuckoo had hopped back into his hole. She looked at the clock, astonished. It was only six! Six in the morning! What a strange time to be playing cricket.

One good thing, her mum and dad would still be safely in bed and asleep and wouldn't see her going down to the garden with Rollsy. She didn't *think* her dad would force her to sell it, although he might if he started worrying about the mortgage. Mum was going to look for another job as soon as Laura had settled in at her new school. She had had a job before but it was too far for her to travel all the way from Turnham Green and so she had had to give it up.

It was all Laura's fault, and by rights Laura *ought* to let Dad sell the Rollsy, except that it didn't really belong to Laura, it belonged to Tommy, and just because Mum and Dad were broke (even though it was because of Laura) that still didn't make it right to sell other people's property.

Laura crept on tiptoe down the stairs, clutching Rollsy in one hand and the banister rail in the other. Silently, stealthily, she stole along the passage and into the kitchen, round the kitchen table (taking care not to knock against the rack where the saucepans were stacked), unhooked the back door key from the hook above the sink, eased open the back door – quietly, quietly! Mum was a light sleeper – and was out at last into the garden.

They were still playing cricket, she could hear the snick of the bat against ball and Tommy's voice crying out that it was "My turn! My turn! I want a go!"

Laura pulled the back door to without actually shutting it and went racing down the garden before her courage could desert her. She wouldn't mind, she thought, if Zilla were there, or her mum; but if it were just Tommy and Em and their dad she might be too shy.

"What do you want to bowl for? You're too little!"

It wasn't Em's voice, and it wasn't Zilla's voice, and yet it sounded familiar. Laura clambered up the timber pile and peered over. Kate, red-headed Kate, was standing there, hands on hips, challenging Tommy. Zilla hadn't said that Kate was coming to stay. Zilla herself wasn't there, and neither were her mum and dad; it was just Tommy and Kate and Em.

Em was batting, standing in front of a wicket chalked on a tree trunk. Her hair was tied neatly in a bunch with a piece of ribbon. She *did* look older than Laura had remembered. She was taller and more gawky, with great gangly legs, and arms that had grown too long for the sleeves of her white blouse, so that her wrists stuck out at the ends.

Laura had heard of people suddenly shooting up. It was what a cousin of hers had done – "She's just suddenly shot up," Laura's gran had said. Laura supposed that it was what Em must have done, and Tommy as well, for Tommy didn't look like a six-year-old any more. He had lost some of his chubbiness and must be very nearly as tall as Laura. Maybe six-year-olds also shot up, though it all seemed to have happened rather fast.

Tommy was still pleading to be allowed to bowl.

"We didn't ask you out here for that," said Kate, tossing the ball from one hand to the other in superior fashion. "You're supposed to be fielding."

"I've *been* fielding! I'm tired of fielding! I want to bowl!"

"Well, you can't," said Kate, "'cos I am."

"Oh, let him have a go if that's what he wants." Em took up her batting position. "Anything to keep him quiet."

"But he can't even bowl overarm!"

"I can!" said Tommy. "I've been practising!"

"Well, I'm not going to field for you." Kate tossed him the ball and stalked off in a huff to sit on the swing. "You'll be knocked all over the place and serve you right."

"Come on, then, Harold Larwood!" Em waved her bat, derisively. "Let's see what you can do."

"Harold Larwood!" Kate sniggered, as she idled to and fro on the swing.

Em said, "All right, then … Bill Voce!" and both girls cackled.

Poor Tommy had turned bright red.

Laura didn't know who Harold Larwood and Bill Voce were – cricketers, she supposed; she didn't know anything about cricket – but it was obvious the two girls were enjoying a laugh at Tommy's expense. Perhaps he would bowl his sister out first ball. Laura found herself rather hoping that he would.

Tommy started his run at the far end of the garden, near the back gate. He charged ferociously towards the wicket, arms flailing like windmills, suddenly stopped dead, whirled his right arm in a circle and let fly with the ball. The ball landed with a flump! in the sandpit. Em rushed forward, flicked it out with her bat and in one swift movement sent it crashing into the trellis.

"Boundary!" chanted Kate, from the swing.

"Do try to get it at least *some*where near the wicket," urged Em.

Scarlet-faced, Tommy retrieved the ball

and trotted back off to start his run again. Laura willed him, this time, to have a better aim.

Tommy charged. His arm whirled, the ball looped up into the air – and hit the earth, *thunk!* a few miserable centimetres away from him. Kate, on her swing, doubled up. Em gave a triumphant howl, tore down the pitch and with one mighty wham! cracked the ball far away into the vegetable patch.

"Six!" gasped Kate, hardly able to speak for laughing.

Well, at least, thought Laura, he would be happy to have his Rollsy back. She wondered whether to give it to him now or wait until he had finished bowling. People only bowled six balls at a time, she knew that much. Six balls was called an over. After that it was someone else's turn.

"You can do it underarm if you'd rather," said Em, kindly.

She made it *sound* kind, but she didn't really mean it kindly, thought Laura. She'd only said it to puncture his little boy's pride. Perhaps she thought Tommy was a bit too pushy, or perhaps he insisted on joining in their games when they didn't really want him and this was their way of punishing him; making him look foolish. Laura thought it was rather mean of Em. If Laura had had a little brother she wouldn't have treated him like that.

Tommy bowled again: once again Em hit him for six.

"Oh, I am enjoying this!" carolled Em.

Laura could see, as Tommy marched back for the fourth time, gripping the ball tightly in his hand, that his face was all scrunched up, trying not to cry. Impulsively she said, "Tommy – " and held out the Rollsy, but he was too intent on showing his sister and red-headed Kate, and didn't hear her.

Charge, went Tommy; straight to the wicket went the ball; *clonk*, went Em, driving it magnificently, up and over the end wall of the garden.

What happened next was a horrible confusion. Tommy turned and went chasing off after the ball at the same time as Kate on her swing drawled, "Em Hobbs has just hit another six." Laura saw Tommy wrench open the back gate. She heard Em's sudden shriek of "Tommy! You come back here this instant! You know you're not allowed out there!"

She saw Em throw down her bat and plunge after him. She heard a squeal of brakes and Em's horrified cry of "Tommeeeee!" She saw Kate jump off the swing and go running. And then there was silence.

Laura stood, petrified, on top of the pile, clinging to the fence post, waiting for the three of them to return. After a few seconds, when they still hadn't done so, she scrambled back down and raced for her own back gate, behind the fir trees. The Leyland cypresses. Her mum and dad had said she wasn't to go out there, but this was an emergency. Brakes had squealed and Em had shouted. And nobody had come back.

Laura wrenched open the gate as far as it would go and squeezed herself out on to the pavement. There she had a shock: the road was completely empty! Not a car, not a lorry, not even a motor bike. And not a sign of the three children.

She stood for a moment, unable to believe it. People couldn't disappear just like that! If there had been an accident, someone would have had to call an ambulance; they wouldn't simply have bundled all three of them into a car and driven off. And if there hadn't been an accident, then why hadn't they come back?

Perhaps they had, and she had missed

them. In through the back gate ran Laura, up again on to the pile –

"Laura!"

That was her mum's voice. Guiltily, Laura sprang round.

"What on earth are you doing out here at this hour? It's only just gone six o'clock!"

"I was awake," said Laura

"Yes, and so was I! I came downstairs to make a cup of tea and found the back door open. Where have you just come from?" A sharp note of inquiry entered her mum's voice. "Laura! You haven't been out of that gate, have you?"

"Not – out, exactly. I just … opened it a little. Just to have a look."

"Why? What for?"

"I thought … I heard something," said Laura. "I thought there'd … been an accident. But there hadn't," she said. "At least, I – I couldn't see anything."

"That's because there wasn't anything *to*

see! You know your trouble, my girl?" Laura's mum put a hand on her shoulder and began firmly to propel her back up the garden towards the house. "You've got too vivid an imagination. I knew this would happen … that Miss Armitage putting ideas into your head!"

Laura wrinkled her brow. "Miss Armitage?"

"The old lady who came to see us – the one who used to come and visit."

"How did she put ideas into my head?"

"Going on about tragic accidents."

"Oh." Laura had forgotten all about Miss Armitage and her tales of bygone days. "Was that what she meant? An accident like – like someone getting run over?"

"I haven't the faintest idea what she meant!" Laura's mum gave her a little push. "Why have you got that toy with you?"

"I – I thought Zilla might be there. I wanted to show it to her."

"At this time in the morning? She'll still be in bed and asleep!"

"*We're* not," said Laura.

"No, that's because one of us listens to things that foolish old ladies tell her and the other one sleeps so lightly she could hear a pin drop. We'll go and have a cup of tea and take ourselves back to bed and get up again at the normal hour. And Laura, don't mention any of this to your dad. It'll only upset him."

Later that day, when Laura's dad was nailing up the back gate and Laura was half-heartedly sieving the earth in her newly-dug flower bed, ready for planting flowers, Zilla's head popped over the fence.

"G-hi!" said Zilla.

"G-hi!" said Laura.

"I'm all right today, I'm standing on a chair."

"That's good," said Laura.

"What are you doing?" Zilla squinted down, trying to see.

"Just digging around," said Laura.

"Do you like gardening? I do. At least, I think I do. I think I *would*. We haven't got a garden where we are. Not a proper one. If we came to live here – "

Zilla paused. Laura went on heaping piles of earth into her sieve.

"My gran's not very well," said Zilla.

"I know," said Laura. "You told me."

"No, but she's worse. She was really bad last night. My mum had to go and sit with her. My dad's going to sit with her tonight. My dad's taking time off work," said Zilla. "He's going to stay here and help look after my gran. He says it's too much for my mum on her own."

Laura made a mumbling noise. She didn't want to hear about Zilla's gran.

"*They're* going to go home," said Zilla.

"Who's they?" said Laura; though of

course she knew quite well.

"*Them*," said Zilla. "My brother and sister."

There was another pause. Laura picked up her sieve in both hands and shook it from side to side. Carelessly she said, "Are they old enough to be by themselves?"

"I should hope so," said Zilla; and she cackled, just like Em.

Laura sat back on her heels. For the first time, she looked directly up at Zilla.

"How old are they, then?"

"My brother's eighteen, my sister's sixteen. He's going to start work soon. *Boring* work. *Insurance* work. She's still at school. She says she's going to be a nurse. Huh! Some nurse! Wouldn't want to be nursed by *her*," said Zilla.

Laura didn't say anything. She thought, this is like when I heard the baby and there wasn't one. She was obviously completely *potty*. She heard babies that didn't exist, she saw children that weren't there. Tommy and Em couldn't possibly be Zilla's brother and sister. So in that case, who were they? And who was Kate?

"I say," said Zilla, "are you all right?"

Laura felt like saying, no, I'm completely potty.

"You looked a bit peculiar for a moment."

Laura thought, I am a bit peculiar. She upended a sieve full of stones into the wheelbarrow.

"Do you think," she said, "that there are people who see things?"

"What, like ghosts and things? Yes, I told you," said Zilla. "My gran does. Why?" She cackled again. "Have you seen one?"

Laura didn't know what she had seen – if indeed she had seen anything. Maybe it was like her mum said, and she just had a vivid imagination. She just *thought* she saw things. And all the time she was making them up.

Perhaps if Zilla came to live here and they went to school together and were friends she wouldn't do it any more. It wasn't any fun seeing things that other people couldn't see and getting your mum and dad all upset so that they took you to doctors and even had to move house. Laura heaved a sigh.

"I wish *I* could see a ghost," said Zilla.

"Why? What would you do?"

"I'd talk to it – I'd ask it questions."

"I don't think ghosts can hear you," said Laura.

"Then I'd write a message for it, like, are you a ghost because something terrible happened to you? Please come back tomorrow and give me the answer."

"How could it?" said Laura.

"Easy! I'd tell it to tuck its head under its arm if the answer was yes and wear it back to front if it was no!"

Silly. Zilla was just being *silly*. You couldn't treat ghosts like that.

Chapter Six

That night in bed was even more horrid than last night had been. Instead of dreaming sad dreams which she forgot as soon as she woke up, Laura kept dreaming of that moment in the garden when Tommy had gone racing through the back gate. She kept hearing Em's scream, and the squeal of brakes. And when she woke up she could still remember it, and all too clearly.

Sternly she reminded herself that Tommy and Em were *not real people*. They were only people she had made up, because of having too vivid an imagination and being an only child and too shy to mix with others. If they had been real people they would still have been there when she went through the back gate, and they hadn't been there, so that proved it.

"Just go back to sleep and don't be a *baby*!" said Laura.

So she went to sleep and dreamed the same horrible dream all over again.

It simply wasn't any use telling herself that Tommy and Em, and red-headed Kate, weren't real: Laura knew otherwise. She wasn't so completely potty that she couldn't tell the difference between real people and made-up people. It was true that she had imaginary friends whom she sometimes played with, and held conversations with, but she *knew* that they were imaginary. They could only talk when Laura made them talk: the other three talked without any prompting at all. And furthermore, they talked of things that Laura knew nothing about. Harold Larwood, for instance, and Bill Voce. Laura had never even heard of Harold Larwood and Bill Voce.

A sudden dismal thought struck her: maybe there weren't any such people? Maybe they were just names that she had invented? Maybe she *was* potty.

The cuckoo hopped out on the end of his spring and cuckooed twelve times. Laura slipped from her bed and went padding up the passage to Mum and Dad's room.

"Dad?" she whispered.

Her dad groaned.

"What is it, Laura?"

"Have you heard of people called Harold Larwood and Bill Voce?"

"Have I heard of – " Her dad shot up in the bed. "What are you asking me that for in the middle of the night?"

"It's only twelve o'clock," said Laura.

"Yes, and I have to be up at six! Just give us a break!"

"Go back to bed," said her mum. "You ought to be asleep."

"But, Dad, *have* you?" said Laura. "Are they real people?"

"They're dead people. Been dead for ages. They were famous cricketers in the nineteen-thirties. Now just get back to your bed and go to sleep!"

Laura trod thoughtfully back to her own room. It was a relief to know that at least they *had* been real people, once, though it was strange that Em should talk about famous cricketers from all that time ago. Surely there were enough famous cricketers of today? Like Ian Botham and – well, Ian Botham was one. There had to be others. If you knew about cricket, that is, which Em appeared to.

Laura crawled back beneath the duvet. She remembered what Miss Armitage had said about a tragic accident. *That* had been a long time ago. Probably as long ago as Harold Larwood and Bill Voce. Suppose Laura had been brave enough to call out and give Tommy his Rollsy before he had started bowling, would the accident still have happened?

He might have been so pleased to have his Rollsy back that he wouldn't have bothered about bowling; he would have left the two girls to get on with it. Did that mean the accident was Laura's fault? That she could have prevented it, if only she hadn't been so silly and shy?

But I tried! thought Laura. I did try! She had called out, and Tommy hadn't heard her, just as Em hadn't when she had been doing her acting.

It was too late to give Tommy his Rollsy back now. Tommy had gone and there was nothing that Laura could do about it. Probably there never had been. After all, the past wouldn't be the past if you could keep going back and altering it.

But the car still didn't belong here, thought Laura, feeling it under her pillow. It belonged in number 42.

I'll take it with me tomorrow, she thought, when I go and have tea with Zilla.

*　*　*

Laura's mum couldn't understand, on Monday afternoon, why Laura wanted to take her shoulder bag with her when she went round to Zilla's.

"I know it's a very *nice* shoulder bag – " it was red canvas, with tassels: Laura's gran had brought it back from holiday – "but you're only going next door!"

"I've got something in it to give to Zilla," said Laura. If her mum asked her what she would say a book; and just to satisfy her conscience she *had* put a book in there. It was one of her Judy Blumes, and she would ask Zilla if she would like to borrow it.

"Well! I don't know," said her mum.

"Even I wouldn't take my handbag just to go next door!"

She seemed to find it amusing, like she had when Laura, in strictest confidence, had suggested that now she was going to secondary school perhaps she ought to wear a bra. Her mum had told her dad about it and they had both laughed. The shame of it was with her still. (Laura had resolved, then, never to trust her mum with a secret again. Grown-ups couldn't be relied on.)

"Don't forget," said her mum, "to ask how Zilla's gran is."

Laura made a mumbling sound.

"It's only polite," said her mum.

Laura waited until she was in the back garden with Zilla. It was easier to ask Zilla than her mum or dad.

"How is your gran?" said Laura.

"She's not very well," said Zilla. "The doctor came this morning. He said maybe she should go into hospital, but my gran doesn't want to go in hospital. She wants to die here."

Laura never knew which way to look when Zilla talked about her gran dying. She made it sound as if it wasn't any different from just going on holiday.

"She's quite ready for it," said Zilla, cheerfully. "She told me. She said, it isn't anything to be scared of."

Laura looked at her, doubtfully.

"It'll be like going on a journey," said Zilla. "That's what my gran says. Just like going on a journey. What do you want to do today? We'd better not play with the roller again 'cos my dad's here. He'd get mad at me. Shall we go down the bottom where they can't see us?"

Laura hesitated. Down the bottom was where the sandpit was, and the swing. It was where the three of them had played, Tommy and Kate and Em.

"Do you want to?" said Zilla.

"Yes, all right," said Laura.

The sandpit wasn't there. She should have been surprised, but nothing surprised her any more. She had given up trying to understand. Where it had been was a patch of scrubby grass with wild flowers. Where the back gate had been, ivy was growing.

"There isn't much down here, really," said Zilla. "My dad said there used to be a swing, once upon a time."

"Over there," said Laura. She pointed. "That's where it was."

Zilla stared. "How d'you know?"

"And there – " Laura swivelled round – "was a sandpit. And there behind the ivy was the back gate, before they got rid of it."

"Who told you that?"

"And over there," said Laura, "were vegetables. Some that climbed up poles, and some like green cauliflowers."

"How do you know?" said Zilla.

Laura looked at her, puzzled. How *did* she know?

"Someone must have told you. That Miss Armitage, I bet. She used to play with my gran when they were young. I bet she told you."

"It was nice, then," said Laura.

"It's quite nice now," said Zilla. "Sort of private ... did you say there was a *sand*pit?"

"Just there," said Laura. She stretched out her leg and touched the edge of the scrubby grass with the tip of her shoe.

"I wouldn't mind some sand," said Zilla, "but I'd like it to be like a beach, with a swimming pool. That'd be brilliant, wouldn't it? If we had a swimming pool? Can you swim? I can, almost. So long as I keep one foot on the bottom. I'm going to learn, next term. My dad's going to teach me. He'll teach you as well, if you like. If we come and live here. That'd be fun, wouldn't it? Both learning to swim together?"

"Yes, it would," said Laura.

When they went in for tea, Zilla's dad was there as well as her mum.

"Dad, could we have a swimming pool?" said Zilla.

"No," said her dad, "is the short answer to that. Hallo, is this Laura? And how is Laura?"

"Very well, thank you," said Laura. She wondered whether it would be polite to ask all over again about Zilla's gran, but fortunately, before she could pluck up courage, Zilla had jumped in again and the moment had passed.

"Laura says there used to be a sandpit at the bottom of the garden."

"Yes, that's right; there did. Who told her that?"

"Miss Armitage," said Zilla.

"Fancy Miss Armitage remembering ... I guess she must have played in it."

"Did you play in it?"

"Me? No! It wasn't there in my time. I just remember seeing photos of it."

"Where?" Zilla sprang up, eagerly. "In the albums? Can I get them out?"

"If you like," said her mum. "They're in the sideboard, but don't disturb all Gran's stuff."

Zilla scampered out of the kitchen, leaving Laura alone with her mum and dad. Laura took a deep breath and, cheeks scarlet, said, "I'm very sorry to hear about Zilla's gran."

"That's sweet of you." Zilla's mum smiled at her across the table. "But she is quite an old lady. I think she feels it's time."

"It comes to us all," said Zilla's dad.

Laura didn't know what to say after that. She was glad when Zilla came racing back carrying a pile of photograph albums, which she dumped breathlessly on the kitchen table.

"Don't look at this top one, this top one's boring, it's just got pictures of us in it … ugh! Look! There's a picture of me!"

Proudly, Zilla shunted a photograph of herself towards Laura.

"Isn't it gruesome? And this one's even gruesomer. This one's *really* gruesome. This one's *them* … my brother and sister. Yuck!"

Laura stared at a photograph of a long thin boy wearing glasses and a rather plump and four-square sort of girl with a brace on her teeth.

"*Chris*topher," said Zilla, "and *Jooo*lia … yeeurgh!"

Zilla made a being-sick noise.

"Stop it!" Her mum slapped at her. "I thought you wanted to look for photographs of the sandpit?"

"Yes! Let's look at the early ones and find the sandpit!"

"OK, then." Zilla's dad pulled one of the

albums towards him and began flicking through it. "There you are ... that's it. That's the one I remember."

"Let's see!" Zilla knelt on a chair beside him, leaning forward with her elbows on the table. "Is that Gran?"

"Yes, that's your gran."

"Laura, look! Do you want to see my gran?"

Laura didn't very much, as a matter of fact. It seemed wrong to be looking at pictures of Zilla's gran as a little girl while as an old lady she lay upstairs dying, but it would have been rude not to show an interest so she slid off her chair and obediently moved round the table next to Zilla.

"There," said Zilla, stabbing a finger.

Laura found herself gazing at a picture of Em and her friend Kate in the sandpit. They were wearing bathing costumes and funny flappy hats like soft bonnets. Em was grinning broadly at the camera; Kate was squinting, because of the sun.

"She was quite pretty," said Zilla, "wasn't she?"

Laura nodded, dumbly.

"I take after her a bit. Everyone says I'm like her. Don't they?" Zilla appealed to her dad. "Doesn't everyone say I'm like Gran?"

"They do," agreed her dad. "There they are again, look, the pair of them … in their Girl Guide uniforms."

"Oh, and look, there's Gran on the swing!"

Em, on the swing, with Kate pushing her. Laura put her finger in her mouth and tore at her finger nail.

"Who's the girl with her?" said Zilla.

Her dad pushed his glasses up his forehead to read what was written under the photographs.

"'Em, with Kate'."

"Who's Kate?"

"Kate Armitage."

"The one who came to visit," said Zilla's mum.

"Oh! Miss Armitage. Incredible! I didn't recognize her. Did you?" Zilla turned to Laura. Laura shook her head. It was true she couldn't see any likeness between lively red-headed Kate and little old white-haired Miss Armitage.

"I doubt if anyone would recognize *you*," said Zilla's mum, "if they saw a picture of you as a baby ... a sweet little thing she was then, Laura."

Laura smiled, but she couldn't help thinking of Em, vivacious bossy Em, bellowing Shakespeare at the top of her voice, whamming cricket balls to the boundary, sculpting sandcastles in the sandpit ... did Zilla's gran remember being young and doing all those things? Did she look back on them as she lay upstairs waiting to die? A shiver went pattering down Laura's spine. She wasn't sure that she liked the thought of growing old.

"Do you think," said Zilla, as she turned the pages, "that Gran remembers all this?"

"I'm sure she does," said Zilla's dad. "In fact, I know she does. She once said to me, that's one of the blessings of old age … you can go back in your memory and re-live all the events from your past."

"Wow!" said Zilla. "That must keep you pretty busy."

She went on, turning the pages. Her dad supplied the commentary.

"That was your gran with her Shakespeare prize … got a prize, she did, for reciting Shakespeare. Always very keen on the acting. I think she might have gone on the stage if she hadn't got married and had me … that old boy there, that's your gran's Uncle Jack. A great character. When I was a kid we still had a rocking horse he'd made. Very clever with his hands, was

Uncle Jack ... and that little chap, that's your gran's brother. The one that got run over. Always troubled your gran, that did; always reckoned for some reason that she was responsible. I never quite got the hang of it, but she's never been easy in her mind."

Zilla's dad sat back in his chair. Laura stood, gazing at the photograph of Tommy.

"She always swears, you know, Laura – " Laura started – "that his ghost still haunts the place."

"Colin, I don't really think –" began Zilla's mum.

"It was a tale I grew up with ... Tommy's ghost. And you know – "

"*Colin* – "

" – the funny thing is, when I was a boy of nine, which is the age he was when he died, I once thought I saw a little kid playing in the garden, down by the vegetable patch, where the sandpit used to be. Of course it was probably only imagination, it never happened again, but – I dunno! It was extraordinarily vivid. I never laugh at people who say they've seen ghosts."

"*Dad!*" Zilla pummelled at him, with her fist. "We're not supposed to talk to Laura about things like that. She gets upset."

"Oh, lor! Have I gone and put my foot in it? I'm sorry, Laura! I'm so used to this little ghoul – " he punched, amiably, at Zilla. "Can't get enough of it, this one ... Dad, Dad, tell me about the ghost! I want to hear about Tommy's ghost! But anyway, even if there are such things, they're perfectly harmless. They can't do anything to you."

"I still maintain," said Zilla's mum, "that it's all a myth. It's all in the mind. Don't you listen to him, Laura! Let's put these silly old photographs away and play a game. What shall we play? We'll have to make something up, we didn't bring any games with us. Zilla, you're good at inventing things. Think of something!"

Zilla's mum cleared the table and they settled down to play a pencil and paper game where everyone had to draw a head, with a neck, and then fold the paper over and pass it to the next person, who drew a body and passed it on to the next person, who drew the legs and passed it on to the last person, who drew the feet.

It was quite fun, but Laura knew they were only playing it to take her mind off Tommy's ghost. She would have liked to tell them it wasn't necessary, that she had seen Tommy, and Em and Kate, all playing in the garden, she had heard them talking, and it wasn't in the least bit scary, they were just like real people; but they probably wouldn't believe her, or if they did, Zilla's mum might feel that she had to pass it on to Laura's mum, and then Laura's mum would get all worried and tell Dad, and Dad would be upset and say, "Oh, Laura, love! We're not starting that again?" It would be best that Mum and Dad didn't know.

When Laura left, she gave Zilla her Judy Blume to read, and gave the Rollsy to Zilla's dad.

"What's this, then?" he said.

"I found it in our garden," said Laura, "but I think it really belongs here."

"Well, I never!" Zilla's dad, just like Laura's, had upended it. "Look at that … *JH, 1924*. That must be old Uncle Jack! It looks like his handiwork. Where did you say you found it, Laura?"

"Under the brambles," said Laura. "Near the escallonia."

"Extraordinary! It must have been there for decades. It certainly wasn't around in my time."

"You won't sell it, will you?" Laura looked at him, anxiously. "It belongs in this house."

"I most certainly won't sell it! Part of family history, this is."

"Gran might recognize it," said Zilla.

"She might, at that. I'll take it up and show her … might jog a few memories. Thank you very much, Laura. What a splendid find!"

Zilla walked with her to the front gate.

"It didn't upset you, did it?" she said. "Dad telling you about Tommy's ghost?"

"Do I look as if I'm upset?" said Laura.

"Well, n-no. I suppose. Except you always look as if you are, a little bit."

"You said I'd freak," said Laura.

"You still might!"

"Well, I won't."

"I do believe in ghosts, actually," said Zilla. "Do you?"

Laura considered. "I suppose it depends what you mean by ghosts."

"Well … *ghosts*," said Zilla. "People that have died and come back to haunt."

"I don't think they necessarily have to have died," said Laura.

"Of course they do! You can't be a ghost and still be alive! How can you be a ghost and still be alive?"

"I think perhaps – " Laura said it carefully, trying to disentangle her thoughts – "I think what it is, I think perhaps we believe in different sorts of ghosts."

"Why? What sort of ghosts do you believe in?"

"I believe in ghosts that are more like … like *memories*," said Laura. "I think that all the time we're here we leave traces of ourselves for other people to pick up, only not many people *can* pick them up, so that when people do, other people either don't believe them and say they're mad or else they say they're seeing ghosts. But it's not that. It's just being able to pick up the traces. At any rate," said Laura, "that's what I believe."

Zilla was looking at her with a new respect.

"You're a dark horse," said Zilla.

Chapter Seven

Laura's dad had just come home from work, and they were about to sit down to their tea, when the front doorbell rang.

"I'll go!" said Laura.

"Not without me," said her mum.

Where they had lived in King's Cross it hadn't always been wise to open your front door in the evening. It was different in Turnham Green, but Laura's mum was still cautious: she always kept the chain on until she knew who it was.

"You can't be too careful," was what

Laura's mum said. She was a very careful person, and Laura took after her. Laura couldn't help wishing, sometimes, that she was a bit more like Zilla. Zilla wouldn't ever bother with bolts and chains. Laura bet Em wouldn't have done, either.

Laura's mum opened the door just a crack, with the chain still on.

"Hallo?" she said.

Zilla and her mum were standing there. Laura's mum took the chain off immediately.

"G-hi!" said Zilla, grinning at Laura.

"G-hi," said Laura.

Laura's mum held open the door.

"Come in," she said, but Zilla's mum shook her head.

"No, no, I'm sure you're in the middle of your tea, I don't want to disturb you. I just wanted to ask you a little favour."

Zilla's mum spoke apologetically. Laura thought, she wants to borrow something.

That was what Mrs Baron, in King's Cross, had meant by a little favour. Mrs Baron had been their neighbour in the flat next door; she had always been "just popping in" to borrow a pint of milk or a packet of tea.

"I wondered if Laura would come in and say hallo to Zilla's gran."

"Laura?" Laura's mum sounded surprised, and slightly startled.

"She's heard so much about her from Zilla … Zilla and her gran chatter away all the time. At least, they used to. They haven't been able to do it so much just recently, her gran's been too ill. But she's heard about Zilla's new friend, and she does so much want to say hallo to her."

"Well – " Laura's mum looked at her, dubiously. "What do you think, Laura?"

"Gran really does want to see you," said Zilla.

"Zilla, sh!" Her mum put her finger to her lips. "It's for Laura to decide. You don't have to if you don't want to, Laura. I shall quite understand. No one's trying to force you."

"That's all right," said Laura. "I don't mind."

She would have minded, this time yesterday; this time yesterday, she would have been terrified. But now she knew that Zilla's gran was Em – well, it was a little bit scary but it wasn't like saying hallo to a complete stranger.

Zilla's mum's face had gone all bright and beaming.

"Are you sure, Laura? Oh, that's marvellous! She'll be so pleased."

"When do you want her to come?" said Laura's mum. Laura's mum still sounded doubtful.

"Would some time this evening be all right? It'll only be a quick in and out … just to say hallo."

They arranged that Laura would call

round as soon as she had had her tea.

"Are you absolutely certain that you want to do this?" said her mum, as they went back to the kitchen to join Laura's dad. "I don't want you getting upset or having one of your funny turns."

"What's this?" said her dad. "What's she going to do?"

"Go next door to say hallo to Zilla's gran."

"The old girl? I thought she was – "

"Yes," said Laura's mum. "She is. But for some reason she wants to say hallo to Laura."

Laura's dad frowned. "Is that a good idea?"

"That's what I'm wondering."

"You know what Laura's like. The least little thing – "

"Mum, please!" said Laura. "I'd like to say hallo."

"But why?" said her mum.

"Well, because – because she wants to!"

And because it seemed only right that Em and Laura should meet each other at last.

"I really would like to," said Laura.

All the same, she had a slight twitch of nerves as she followed Zilla's mum up the stairs. Em wasn't going to be the Em who played in the garden and acted Shakespeare. That Em had disappeared a long time ago. This Em was going to be an old lady who was dying, and Laura suddenly felt that it might be rather frightening. She had never seen a person who was dying before.

"Mother?" said Zilla's mum, opening the bedroom door. "I've brought Laura to see you … Zilla's friend."

Laura crept into the bedroom behind Zilla's mum. An old lady lay in the bed, propped against the pillows. She was tiny and shrunken, with wispy white hair as fine as a baby's, but when she opened her eyes Laura knew that she was Em. The eyes were the same eyes, brown and brilliant, which had looked straight through Laura on the day when Em had been doing her acting.

The old lady let a hand crawl out across the bed. Laura touched it, very gently, with the tips of her fingers. The skin was so thin it was almost transparent; she felt that if she were to do more than just brush it, it might tear.

"So you're ... the little ... girl who ... found ... Tommy's ... toy."

Laura crouched down, so that her head was on a level with Em's.

"I saw it come over the fence – I saw you throw it. Then I – I saw you climb over!"

The ghost of a smile uplifted one corner of Em's mouth.

"I was ... a tomboy in ... those ... days."

"I looked for it for you," said Laura, "but it wasn't until Dad cut the brambles that I found it."

"Tommy will be ... so glad ... to have it ... again. God bless you ... my dear."

The old lady's eyes closed. There was a pause, then Zilla's mum quietly beckoned Laura from the room.

"Thank you so much, Laura," she whispered. "I can't tell you ... such a difference! The minute she saw the toy. She won't be parted from it – she insists on having it under her pillow."

Laura nodded. Under the pillow was the best place for it.

"What did you mean," said Zilla's mum, as she closed the door, "when you said you saw it come over the fence?"

"I saw it happen," said Laura, "all those years ago."

"You saw it *happen*?"

"Yes," said Laura. "But you can't do anything about it at the time."

"Well, you've done something about it now." Zilla's mum studied her for a

moment then smiled encouragingly and
squeezed her hand. "You've made one old
lady very happy."

*   *   *

That night, Laura fell asleep the minute she
turned out the light and slept without
waking right round until morning.

"Thank heavens for that!" said her mum,
next day at breakfast. "Your dad wasn't best
pleased at being woken up at twelve o'clock
the other night, I can tell you!"

"I know, but I had to find out," said
Laura.

"Find out what?"

"Find out – " What was it she had had
to find out? "Find out who those people
were."

Already she had forgotten their names. It
didn't seem to matter any more.

"Well, I'm glad you've had a good night,"
said her mum. "I was starting to get
worried."

"There wasn't any need," said Laura. "Honestly."

Later that morning, Zilla and her mum called round. Laura's mum invited them in for a coffee.

"I just came to let you know," said Zilla's mum, "that Zilla's gran passed away peacefully last night in her sleep."

Laura's mum shot a quick troubled glance at Laura.

"Do you two girls want to go and play in the garden?"

"She thinks I'll be upset," said Laura, as she and Zilla wandered out into the sunshine.

"Why?" said Zilla. "She wasn't your gran. You didn't even know her."

"I did, sort of," said Laura.

"Not like I did," said Zilla. Two fat tears spilled out of Zilla's eyes and went rolling down her cheeks.

"She was my gran," said Zilla.

"Yes, I know," said Laura.

There was an awkward silence. Zilla sniffed, rather fiercely, and scrubbed at her eyes with the sleeve of her cardigan.

"All right, so let's play something!"

"What shall we play?"

"Anything!"

"I'll get a ball, shall I, and we'll play catching?"

Laura went running off to fetch one. When she came back, Zilla was clambering about in the boughs of the apple tree.

"Hey! It's great up here!"

"Come down," said Laura, "and we'll play."

Zilla plopped down on to the grass.

"My gran was happy," she said. "She was just waiting to go. I bet she's meeting all those people that she used to know ... I bet she's saying hallo to them right now."

"I bet," said Laura. She threw the ball. "Here! Catch! I've invented a new game ...

first of all we stand *close* – "

First of all they stood close – so close they were touching – and simply passed the ball between them; then they took a step backwards, and then another, and then another, until in the end – "So long as we don't drop it, 'cos if we drop it we have to go back and start again" – Zilla was going to be right up by the house and Laura down by the Leyland cypresses.

Of course they didn't get that far – they couldn't have thrown that far. They started off by the apple tree, because that was more or less in the middle, and Laura had just reached the timber pile, while Zilla was level with the escallonia, when one of Zilla's balls went wide, flying high out of reach over Laura's head towards the Hobbs's garden next door. Laura turned and scurried after it, up the pile. And as she did so, she heard Em's voice.

"Oh, I am enjoying this!" carolled Em.

Laura froze. She heard the familiar sound of bat on ball, she heard Kate's voice, lazily drawling, "Em Hobbs has just hit another six." She heard Tommy crashing through the bushes, heard the back gate being pulled open, heard Em's sudden horrified shriek of "Tommy! You come back here this instant!"

It was all happening, all over again.

Laura crouched, trembling, waiting for the squeal of brakes – but this time the squeal of brakes never came. Instead she heard Em call, "Tommee! Wait for me! I'm coming!" and Tommy's voice in reply, taunting her, "Catch me if you can! Bet you can't catch me!"

"*Tommee* – "

"Catch me, catch me, c –"

And then there was a squeal, but it wasn't brakes, it was Tommy being caught by Em. She knew that Em had caught him because she could hear him giggling in between the squeals.

Slowly, Laura stood up and looked over the fence into next door's garden. It was just as she had seen it yesterday, with Zilla. Where the sandpit had been was now a bed of scrubby grass, with wild flowers growing. The swing had gone; the children weren't there any more. But faintly, in the distance, she could hear the sound of Tommy's giggles, and Em's voice raised, mock scolding: "You rotten little beast! I'll show you!"

She knew, then, that Tommy and Em were together again.

"Hey!" Zilla came pounding up the garden. "What are you doing?"

"Just looking for the ball," said Laura. She snatched it up and flung it at Zilla. "*Catch!*"

Hippo Fantasy

Lose yourself in a whole new world, a world where anything is possible – from wizards and dragons, to time travel and new civilizations ... Gripping, thrilling, scary and funny by turns, these Hippo Fantasy titles will hold you captivated to the very last page.

The Night of Wishes
Michael Ende (author of *The Neverending Story*)

It's New Year's Eve, and Beelzebub Preposteror, sorceror and evil-doer, has only seven hours to complete his annual share of villainous deeds and *completely destroy the world!*

Rowan of Rin
Emily Rodda

The witch Sheba has made a mysterious prophecy, which is like a riddle. A riddle Rowan must solve if he is to find out the secret of the mountain and save Rin from disaster ...

The Wednesday Wizard
Sherryl Jordan

Denzil, humble apprentice to the wizard Valvasor, is in a real pickle. When he tries to reach his master to warn him of a dragon attack, he mucks up the spell and ends up seven centuries into the future!

The Practical Princess
Jay Williams

The Practical Princess has the gift of common sense. And when you spend your days tackling dragons and avoiding marriage to unsuitable suitors, common sense definitely comes in useful!

HIPPO ANIMAL STORIES

*If you like animals, then you'll love
Hippo Animal Stories!*

Look out for:

Animal Rescue by Bette Paul

Tessa finds life in the country *so* different from life in
the town. Will she ever be accepted? But everything
changes when she meets Nora and Ned who run the
village animal sanctuary, and becomes involved in a
struggle to save the badgers of Delves Wood
from destruction . . .

Thunderfoot by Deborah van der Beek

Mel Whitby has always loved horses, and when she
comes across an enormous but neglected horse in a
railway field, she desperately wants to take care of it.
But little does she know that taking care of
Thunderfoot will change her life forever . . .

A Foxcub Named Freedom
by Brenda Jobling

A vixen lies seriously injured in the undergrowth. Her
young son comes to her for comfort and warmth. The
cub wants to help his mother to safety, but it is
impossible. The vixen, sensing danger, nudges him
away, caring nothing for herself – only for
his freedom . . .

by R.L. Stine

Reader beware, you're in for a scare!

These terrifying tales will send shivers up your spine . . .

Available now:

Our favourite Babysitters are detectives too! Don't miss the new series of Babysitters Club Mysteries:

Available now:

No 1: Stacey and the Missing Ring
When Stacey's accused of stealing a valuable ring from a new family she's been sitting for, she's devastated – Stacey is *not* a thief!

No 2: Beware, Dawn!
Just *who* is the mysterious "Mr X" who's been sending threatening notes to Dawn and phoning her while she's babysitting, *alone?*

No 3: Mallory and the Ghost Cat
Mallory thinks she's solved the mystery of the spooky cat cries coming from the Craine's attic. But Mallory can *still* hear crying. Will Mallory find the *real* ghost of a cat this time?

No 4: Kristy and the Missing Child
When little Jake Kuhn goes missing, Kristy can't stop thinking about it. Kristy makes up her mind. She *must* find Jake Kuhn . . . wherever he is!

No 5: Mary Anne and the Secret in the Attic
Mary Anne is curious about her mother, who died when she was just a baby. Whilst rooting around in her creepy old attic Mary Anne comes across a secret she never knew . . .

Look out for:

No 6: The Mystery at Claudia's House
No 7: Dawn and the Disappearing Dogs
No 8: Jessi and the Jewel Thieves
No 9: Kristy and the Haunted Mansion
No 10: Stacey and the Mystery Money

The Babysitters Club

Need a babysitter? Then call the Babysitters Club. Kristy Thomas and her friends are all experienced sitters. They can tackle any job from rampaging toddlers to a pandemonium of pets. To find out all about them, read on!